UNKNOWN MASTERPIECES

UNKNOWN MASTERPIECES

WRITERS REDISCOVER LITERATURE'S HIDDEN CLASSICS

Edited by
EDWIN FRANK

NEW YORK REVIEW BOOKS

New York

This is a New York Review Book
Published by The New York Review of Books
1755 Broadway, New York, NY 10019

Library of Congress Cataloging-in-Publication Data
Unknown masterpieces : writers rediscover literature's hidden classics /
edited by Edwin Frank.
    p. cm. — (New York Review Books classics)
  ISBN 1-59017-077-6 (alk. paper)
  1. Literature, Modern—19th century—History and criticism. 2.
Literature, Modern—20th century—History and criticism. I. Frank,
Edwin, 1960- II. Series.
  PN761.U55 2003
  809'.03—dc21
                                    2003009583

ISBN-13: 978-1-59017-077-9
ISBN-10: 1-59017-077-6

Book design by Lizzie Scott
Printed in the United States of America on acid-free paper.
10 9 8 7 6 5 4 3

www.nyrb.com

CONTENTS

PREFACE

THE THIRTEEN contributors to this collection write about extraordinary, beautiful, important books that they care about deeply and feel are less well known than they should be. Why these books are not better known is worth a moment's thought.

Consider, for example, the case of Richard Hughes's *A High Wind in Jamaica*. Hughes's novel tells the story of a group of none-too-successful pirates—tired men who go on cruising the backwaters of the Caribbean on the lookout for what small loot they can come by largely because they are too unimaginative and too unenterprising to do anything else, a gang more pathetic than appalling—who one day, quite inadvertently, find that they have abducted a whole family of nice English children. What to do? The pirates can't (or at least won't) get rid of the children, so they do their best to take care of them while hoping to find some way at some point to get them off their hands. But of course the longer the children and the pirates are together, the more they are implicated in each other's existence and the more they are compromised by their shared histories. Things do not end well.

What makes Hughes's story so memorable is that his particular ship of fools unexpectedly becomes a sly but potent figure for all the weird dependency, destructiveness, and incomprehension vexing the relations of children and adults. And not just adults—this is the secret burden behind a tale of children forcibly separated from their parents—but specifically parents and children.

The book is short and everywhere striking. It depicts, in highly ingenious form, the treacherous and inescapable dynamics of the family romance. It has, in other words, both the originality and the universality of a classic, and it had the good fortune in its own day, the 1920s, of being a bestseller. Why then, seventy-five years later, was it more or less forgotten? The reason, I suspect, is as simple as it is unjust: the book is absolutely singular, it belongs to a class of one—nothing else before or after had its mixture of sophistication and almost savage fantasy. So though a success, *A High Wind in Jamaica* was without successors—finding no writers to echo it, no professors to profess it—and without successors a name doesn't survive.

Except of course Richard Hughes's book has. It has survived, as books will do, whether on the shelves of libraries, private and public, or in boxes in attics or on tables at yard sales, on the crammed shelves of second-hand shops, or in the messiest storehouse of all, memory, until picked up again by a curious child or an idle adult and given a chance to reexert their charm and reestablish their command. And it is this survival that the essays gathered here celebrate and strive to ensure. First and foremost, they celebrate the particular enterprise of the authors discussed and, of course, the distinctive virtues—whether of writing or plotting, dialogue or character—of their particular books. They celebrate too, at least implicitly, the unexpected opportunity of meeting with the unknown that books hold out to us. And then they pay tribute to the sheer stubborn staying-power of the book, as both imaginative act and physical fact. "Those of us who love books," Michael Cunningham says with regard to Glenway Wescott's *The Pilgrim Hawk*, "as well as those of us who write them, are sometimes called upon for prodigious acts of patience." An unspoken subtext of the essays here has to be the role played by the book itself—inked paper compactly bound together, produced in some quantity (even if only one), small enough to keep or hide or overlook or carry off—in making sure that so much that might have been lost continues to "dwell in possibility."

If I have dwelt on Hughes's *A High Wind in Jamaica*— the special magic and terror of which Francine Prose's essay in this collection goes so much further to convey—it is not only because the history of its reception seems illustrative of the perils that good books may confront, but also because it was one of the first books in the Classics series published by New York Review

Books, which has just now reached its hundredth title. All of the essays in this book were commissioned by my colleagues Kerry Fried and Amy Loyd and by me as introductions to books in the series, and all of the books under consideration here share, however differently in each case, something of the singularity, the stubborn oddness, of Hughes's novel, as well as its uncertain fortunes.

Max Beerbohm, for example—John Updike's subject here—was a master of the comic sketch, while William Roughhead was a master of the true crime story (a denizen, as Luc Sante remarks, of literature's back alleys). The very high art of both writers has been neglected because they worked in what are considered low, suspect genres. Stendhal's pseudonymous account of his childhood, *The Life of Henry Brulard*, which unites a blistering denunciation of his father with an incestuous homage to his mother, was unpublishable in his day, though the author himself had it bound with costly illustrations stitched in among its pages to prevent it from being discarded on discovery. It is something of a miracle that we have it to read now. As for L. P. Hartley's great novel *The Go-Between*, it remains underappreciated, certainly in America, because it looked old-fashioned when it came out in the early 1950s. With time, however, it has become clear that what might be dismissed as a Victorian novel in modern guise might also be thought a modern novel in Victorian guise. *The*

Go-Between is as beautiful and moving as it is because it dramatizes that ambivalence, so that everything in it is shot through, like watered silk, with its strange shimmer.

Masterpiece, classic—these thirteen books have every right to those titles, and yet in a sense they are misrepresented by them. Masterpieces are showpieces, designed to establish a public reputation; classics (when not a label slapped on cheap shoes or oversized cookies) constitute the public face of knowledge, the books that everyone should know. But for the most part the books discussed in this volume belong to what might be called literature's farther reaches, a more private realm where looming landmarks are of less account than the blazings of particular readers. This privacy, as much as the publicity enjoyed by the famous, can be a complicated, demanding thing. Balzac's *The Unknown Masterpiece* suggests that a great artist's work may finally prove to be in a language so private as to be indistinguishable from nonsense, and it is not impossible to imagine a brilliant reader who becomes exclusively attached to purely banal or esoteric texts, discerning a beauty there that no one else can see. But then one of the implications of Balzac's teasing fable is that our attachment to art—all those things we claim not to know much about but know we like—depends as much on our being able to find something to say in response to it as it does on the supposedly simple evidence of our senses. No one disputes the fine points of natural beauty—waterfall, wildflower—but books of any sort are sustained less through universal acclamation than through the excited, often contradictory, exchanges of their readers.

Happily there is plenty talked about—and plenty to go on talking about—in the essays that follow, each a specific, partisan response of a writer and critic to the work of another writer. If they turn heads, as one hopes they do, it should be to provoke some argument as well. Each makes a case, tries to show what works and what matters, for the author, for us, in the book at hand. Toni Morrison offers a new reading of Camara Laye's *The Radiance of the King* together with a critique of the image of Africa in literature. Arthur Danto turns his attention to the sexual dynamics in Balzac's *The Unknown Masterpiece*. James Wood, in his essay on Shchedrin's *The Golovlyov Family*, considers the shifting features of literary hypocrisy. And the collection as a whole, I'd hope, like the New York Review Books series to which it might be considered an introduction, also makes a larger case about the unexpected ways in which the past may lighten the burden of the present.

Here I'm reminded of some remarks of the maverick Welsh artist and poet David Jones—often set beside Pound and Joyce as the "lost great modernist"—whose beautiful and terrifying account of his experience as an infantryman in World War I, *In Parenthesis*, has just been reprinted by New York Review Books (with an introduction by W. S. Merwin). Jones worked in almost complete obscurity for many years, receiving little public recognition until he was quite old. His work was, and remains, like much of the other work here, lonely. Applying late in life for assistance from a foundation, Jones wrote:

> In our present megalopolitan technocracy the artist must still remain a "rememberer" (part of the official bardic function in earlier phases of society). But in the totally changed and rapidly changing circumstances of today this ancient function takes on a peculiar significance. For now the artist becomes, willy-nilly, a sort of Boethius, who has been nicknamed "the Bridge," because he carried forward into an altogether metamorphosed world certain of the fading oracles which had sustained antiquity.... When asked to what end does my work proceed I can do no more than answer in the most tentative and hesitant fashion imaginable, thus: Perhaps it is in the maintenance of some sort of single plank in some sort of bridge.

This was 1959, and the statement now seems, in interesting ways, dated: "megalopolitan technocracy" sounds faded, even somewhat hapless, as impatient words later tend to (not that that detracts from their original justice or necessity). By this time, too, for better or for worse, Boethius has become a remote figure indeed, though it might be curious to set *On the Yard*, which Malcolm Braly wrote in San Quentin and about which Jonathan Lethem writes here, beside the ancient prisoner's dialogues with Dame Philosophy. And yet to notice these things, and the alert, shifting tenor of Jones's words, is to notice the struggle with history that is going on within them, as in any considered words. Meanwhile, however, almost off-handedly, a metaphor emerges—of the individual artist's work as part of a great bridge, spanning everywhere and nowhere, its foundations lost in time—that is modest, exact, and marvelous. The pieces in this book are an invitation to cross over.

—EDWIN FRANK

UNKNOWN MASTERPIECES

Eliot Weinberger on

HINDOO HOLIDAY

BY J. R. ACKERLEY

THE DOUBLE "o" in the title immediately signals that we are returning to another time: one that was not so long ago, but is now as antiquated as its orthography. An era that was tragic, perhaps, in its essence, but comic in its particulars; a time of unspeakable wealth and inconceivable poverty, continual cultural misunderstandings, unfettered whimsy, and cruelties large and small: the age of the British Raj and the Indian princes.

The Raj was born in the wake of the 1857 Sepoy Revolt against the Honourable East India Company, which had controlled much of the subcontinent for a hundred years. Realizing that the Company could no longer protect British interests, the British government, with some reluctance, intervened. Slightly more than half of the country fell under the direct administration of the Crown, but the rest of the land was divided into 562 states, from tiny principalities to kingdoms as large as the British Isles themselves. These states enjoyed varying degrees of autonomy in their internal affairs, but all had to pledge not to pursue independent courses of foreign policy.

3

This meant peace for hundreds of kingdoms that had spent centuries warring. And it meant that the princes, whose pride was based on a heritage of martial valor, had to find new ways of demonstrating their princeliness. Many found the solution in the overflowing coffers of their treasuries. With war no longer draining their time and revenues, they attacked leisure as though it were the citadel of an ancient rival.

There were palaces with seven thousand servants, and a maharani whose jewels were so heavy she could stand only when supported by two attendants. There were royal hunts on the backs of four hundred elephants, where scores of tigers or tens of thousands of birds would be slain in a single day. There were children's toys of solid gold, nursery balls encrusted with rubies, a turban with three thousand diamonds, a carpet made only of jewels.

There was a maharajah who changed his clothes when the thermometer rose or fell by one degree, and one who sent his laundry to Paris. There was an auto enthusiast with 270 cars for his personal motoring, and a Scotophile who outfitted his idle troops in complete Highland gear (with the addition of pink tights, so that the brown knees of his men would take on a ruddy Scots complexion). There was one, unlucky in love, who checked into a Paris hotel, ordered cases of Dom Perignon, and drank until he died. And another who occupied thirty-five suites of the Savoy in London and received three thousand fresh roses a day, for he said he loved nature.

A fantastic spire atop the most hierarchical society in the East, princely India was administered or advised by the stodgy, lower-middle-class members of the military and bureaucratic castes of the most hierarchical society in the West. Transformed by colonialism into aristocrats, these sahibs and memsahibs inhabited a world of pig-sticking and costume balls, puttees and topees, tin peas and quinine, calling cards and chits. A world that was ritualized in its slightest details to preserve its newly found decorum in the vastness of an India teeming with germs and masses: a chaos to be largely ignored but strictly controlled when it entered the home or barracks or office in the form of the retinues of servants.

J. R. Ackerley wandered into this scene in 1923. The handsome son of an extravagantly *nouveau riche* fruiterer—the self-styled "Banana King of London"—he had gone directly from his militaristic public school into the trenches soon after war was declared in 1914. He saw action at the Somme (where a million and a half shells were fired, and sixty thousand British soldiers were killed or wounded on the first day) and in other terrible battles; lost his idolized brother; was wounded and taken prisoner; and was not returned to England until months after the peace.

He then entered Cambridge, and a homosexual world that itself now seems as remote as the Raj. Still under the shadow of the Oscar Wilde trial and the Sodomy Laws, more circumspect than closeted, it was a tiny universe of brilliant upper-class men who reveled and suffered under a sharp class distinction between sex and friendship. As detailed in Peter Parker's witty biography of Ackerley, they talked endlessly to each other about their sex lives, but would select their actual partners from the working class. Often heterosexual and sometimes married, their lovers—unlike themselves—had little spare time and little to say that would be of interest to Oxbridge. Romance was furtive, brief, complicated to arrange, thrilling, and boring.

In 1923, Ackerley was twenty-seven, had published a few poems, had written a play, *The Prisoners of War*, that was having trouble finding a producer because of its implicit homoeroticism, and was adrift. His friend E. M. Forster suggested a stint in India, from which Forster had recently returned, perhaps as the secretary to the Maharajah of Chhatarpur, a minor noble whom he called "the Prince of Muddlers, even among Indian muddlers"—and who was also gay.

Months of negotiation followed. The Maharajah had wanted a secretary who was exactly like Olaf, a character in H. Rider Haggard's *The Wanderer's Necklace*, and had even written to Haggard for help. He was oddly unimpressed by Ackerley's photograph, then impressed by his poems, offered him lifetime employment leading to a cabinet post, dismissed the whole thing as impossible, and finally hired him for six months. Ackerley ended up staying less than five.

Back in England, Ackerley slowly transformed his Indian diaries into *Hindoo Holiday*, which appeared in 1932. His publisher, fearful of libel, had insisted on cuts in the text pertaining to the Maharajah's sexual preferences and speculations on the paternity of his heirs. Chhatarpur was jokingly changed to Chhokrapur, which means "City of Boys." Nevertheless, it was too salacious to be broadcast on the BBC, and salacious enough to become an instant and unexpected hit. Vita Sackville-West, Evelyn Waugh, and Cyril Connolly loved it. André Gide recommended it to Gallimard, and the Aga Khan, the playboy spiritual leader of the Ismailis, not only insisted on writing a preface to the French edition but also named a race horse after the book. (Unfortunately it was a loser.) The book remained in print for decades. A new edition in 1952 restored some of the cuts, but it was not, strangely, until its first Indian edition in 1979 that readers could find a completely unexpurgated text. (This is the first Western edition of the uncut version.)

Ackerley went on to become the much-loved literary editor of *The Listener* from 1935 to 1959, and to write, at tortoise pace, three more books: an extraordinary portrait of his Alsatian, *My Dog Tulip* (1956); an autobiographical novel, *We Think the World of You*, which was rejected by Maurice Girodias as "not dirty enough" but which became a scandalous prize winner; and the frank and pioneering memoir *My Father and Myself*, which Ackerley had begun in 1933 and finished just before his death in 1967.

V. S. Naipaul, recalling his first visit to India (in *The Enigma of Arrival*), writes:

> India was special to England; for two hundred years there had been any number of English travelers' accounts and, latterly, novels. I could not be that kind of traveler. In traveling to India I was traveling to an un-English fantasy, and a fantasy unknown to Indians of India.... There was no model for me here, in this exploration; neither Forster nor Ackerley nor Kipling could help.

It is an indication of the place that *Hindoo Holiday* held on the short shelf of enduring literary books produced by the Raj: preceded only by Emily Eden's *Up the Country* in the mid-nineteenth century, and, of course, by *Kim* and *A Passage to India*. Later it was followed by L. H. Myers's *The Root and the Flower* (also known as *The Near and the Far*, a tetralogy of philosophical novels set in the Mughal age, and thus a product of the Raj but not about it) and Paul Scott's operatic *The Raj Quartet* with its nostalgic coda, *Staying On*. The literature's final flowering was, appropriately, not written by an Englishman, but by a fiercely Anglophilic Bengali, Nirad C. Chaudhuri, in his half-Proustian, half-polemical *Autobiography of an Unknown Indian*.

Hindoo Holiday is the most comic of these, and the only one to avoid larger issues, eternal mysteries, or the temptation to throng with as much life as India itself. Ackerley was clearly severe in reworking his diaries, limiting himself to the creation of a handful of unforgettable characters, and eliminating anything he experienced outside of Chhatarpur itself. There is no description of his journey to the state, and none of his departure; a three-week trip to Benares and other places is discussed only in terms of the complex negotiations with the Maharajah for a leave; and there is no mention of the famed erotic temples of Khajaraho, which were nearby and which he surely visited. Instead, he essentially transplanted the comedy of manners from an English country estate to an Indian palace; this may be the only travel book ever written that could easily be adapted as a play.

Ackerley makes no pretense that this is anything more than a holiday; he does not presume to characterize, let alone condemn, the Indian soul, based on his chance encounters. (And in fact he is often a little fuzzy or simply wrong on Indian details.) Kipling loved India, and especially the words of Anglo-India—the first half of *Kim* has an exuberance of language that would not be seen again until Joyce—but he still bore the white man's burden. Ackerley, even more than Forster, has no agenda; both are extraordinarily tolerant, reserving their scorn —like many travelers—only for their fellow countrymen.

That this was due to their lives as sexual outsiders is unquestionable. Although it seems unimaginable now— given the prudishness, until quite recently, of modern India, with its covered and secluded women, and where even a kiss was forbidden on a movie screen—it was sexual licentiousness that was at the root of the Raj's horror of the land. The biggest-selling book on India before *Hindoo Holiday* was Katherine Mayo's 1927 *Mother India*, which claimed that the "degeneracy" of the Indian race was due not to poverty or the tyrannies of its various rulers, but rather to promiscuity:

> The whole pyramid of Indians' woes, material and spiritual—poverty, sickness, ignorance, political minority, melancholy, ineffectiveness, not forgetting that subconscious conviction of inferiority which he forever bares and advertises by his gnawing and imaginative alertness for social affronts— rests upon a rockbottom physical base. The base is simply, his manner of getting into the world and his sex-life thenceforward.

Even worse than sex, of course, was interracial sex: it is the enigma around which *A Passage to India* turns, and the revulsion of it propels the violence of *The Raj Quartet*. In contrast, the one kiss in *Hindoo Holiday* is merely a funny and sweet moment of no significance. The Maharajah's pursuit of his boy actors is presented as comically as his long drives in search of good omens, or the tutor Abdul's pursuit of better employment. Ackerley's descriptions of the beauties of the boys he sees are as relaxed and natural as his descriptions of wildlife; they are entirely without the psychodrama or the Hellenistic pretensions that were common among gay writers at the time. This offhand and funny presentation of the potentially shocking would become an Ackerley trademark. *My Father and Myself* famously begins: "I was born in 1896 and my parents were married in 1919."

No English writer had such uncomplicated fun in India; none could create such comic characters without condescension; no one, until Salman Rushdie and the current generation of Indian novelists, could write dialogue in Indian English so well. Above all, *Hindoo Holiday* is as perfectly constructed as *A Passage to India*, though because of its pose as a travel book and not a novel, few seemed to have noticed.

Arthur C. Danto on

THE UNKNOWN MASTERPIECE
BY HONORÉ DE BALZAC

I think a man spends his whole lifetime painting one picture or working on one piece of sculpture. The question of stopping is really a decision of moral considerations. To what extent are you intoxicated by the actual act, so that you are beguiled by it? To what extent are you charmed by its inner life? And to what extent do you then really approach the intention or desire that is really outside it? The decision is always made when the piece has something in it that you wanted.

— BARNETT NEWMAN

THE EVENTS of human life, be they public or private," Balzac wrote, "are so intimately bound up with architecture, that the majority of observers can reconstruct nations or individuals in the full reality of their behavior, from the remnants of their public monuments or the examination of their domestic remains." The novel in which this passage appears—*The Pursuit of the Absolute*—thus begins with a description of a specific house in a specific street in a specific town: a lodging in the rue de Paris in Douai, "the physiognomy, the interior disposition, and the details of which have, more than any of the other houses, retained the character of the old Flemish buildings, so naively appropriate to the patriarchal mores of that good country." And the action of the novel unfolds along the lines our social intuitions have been prompted by the architecture to anticipate. Here, as elsewhere in his vast work, Balzac sets down, with the precision of a journalistic dispatch, the *coordonnées* of place, time, history, and politics against which his stories are plotted, as a way to give his dreamlike inventions the possibility of human truth.

The sites of Balzac's fictions are nearly always real places, but so transfigured that the house at 7, rue des Grands-Augustins in Paris, where the action of *The Unknown Masterpiece* begins, belongs as much if not more to his great character, the painter Frenhofer, as to Picasso, who took it for his studio in 1937, almost certainly because he believed it to have been where Frenhofer's story was set.[1] And Frenhofer himself is so close to the limits of true artistic creativity as to have become part of the self-image of every artist familiar with him. There is a famous passage in Émile Bernard's recorded conversations with Cézanne, in which the aging master explicitly identifies with Balzac's painter:

---

1. In Balzac's novel, of course, it is the studio of the painter François Porbus; Frenhofer's is "near the Pont St. Michel," a few streets away, near where Matisse, himself an admirer of Frenhofer, was to have a studio on the Quai St. Michel through the 1920s. Picasso executed a suite of etchings based on *Le Chef-d'oeuvre inconnu* in 1927 for the dealer Ambroise Vollard, who published them in 1931 to mark the centenary of the novel. His own masterpiece, *Guernica*, was painted in the rue des Grands-Augustins.

One evening when I was speaking to him about *The Unknown Masterpiece* and of Frenhofer, the hero of Balzac's drama, he got up from the table, planted himself before me, and, striking his chest with his index finger, designated himself—without a word, but through this repeated gesture—as the very person in the story. He was so moved that tears filled his eyes.[2]

Frenhofer is, as Balzac explicitly notes in connection with his musical counterpart, the obsessed composer Gambara, a figure out of E. T. A. Hoffmann's *Tales*. Both stories are niched in that arrondissement of *La Comédie humaine* which he designates *Études philosophiques*—fictional exercises in which "the ravages of thought are depicted." Balzac himself, one might say, is made of the same fabric as his artists—a pilgrim in quest of the Absolute. *La Comédie humaine* was no more realizable as a whole than Frenhofer's painting or Gambara's perfect symphony. To any of these artists we can apply the brilliant witticism with which Jean Cocteau characterized Balzac's friend and admirer, Victor Hugo: that he was a madman who believed he was Victor Hugo. Balzac was a madman who actually lived a life that would strain

---

2. In an interview with J. Gasquet, Cézanne makes the same identification, somewhat less emotively. He describes the way his eyes remain so attached to the painting he is working on that it feels as if they might bleed. "Am I not somewhat crazy? Fixated on my painting [like] Frenhofer?"

credulity had he written the story of it as a fiction. We as much believe in Frenhofer—unlike any of Hoffmann's characters—as we believe in Balzac himself as a kind of true impossibility.

It says something about the power of Balzac's fiction that Frenhofer remains more real to us than either of the two historical artists—Nicolas Poussin and Franz Pourbus—who interact with him in *The Unknown Masterpiece*. Or perhaps it is a tribute to the fact that the highly romanticized vision of art and especially of painting, through which Balzac imagined Frenhofer and his *chef-d'oeuvre*, remains, even in this age of cynicism and deconstruction, the strongest component in our concept of art and certainly our concept of painting, whereas it is all but impossible to see Poussin's austerely intellectual canvases, let alone the late Mannerist compositions of the court painter Franz Pourbus—for whom Balzac employs the gallicized name Porbus[3]—in such terms. They are reimagined by Balzac for the purposes of his story— but Frenhofer has, unlike either of them, become a living myth. Poussin and Pourbus are too locked into the history of art to be successfully reimagined, though it is true that Balzac somewhat transforms them for purposes of his parable.

The story is set in the Left Bank of Paris, on a chill

---

3. In order to avoid confusion, I shall use "Pourbus" to refer to the actual painter, and "Porbus" to refer to Balzac's somewhat fictionalized character based on Pourbus.

December afternoon in 1612. In art-historical truth, Poussin indeed arrived in Paris in 1612 at the age of eighteen, but though he was to become the greatest French painter of his age, in reality he was hardly the prodigy Balzac depicts, dashing off a drawn copy of Porbus's painting in a matter of minutes, and signing it as an advertisement for himself. According to the leading Poussin expert of the twentieth century, Anthony Blunt, "In an age of virtuosi, [Poussin] was a plodder." His "earliest surviving works show that at the age of thirty he had hardly attained the skill that would have been expected from a youth of eighteen in the academic studios of Rome and Bologna." The Flemish master Franz Pourbus the Younger was in his early forties in 1612, and, as Balzac's story implies, he was exceedingly successful as the leading portraitist of his era and, in particular, as the official portraitist of Marie de Medici, Queen Mother and Regent of France. He introduced into French art the grand manner of Venetian design, which he had mastered during a long residence in Italy, at the Court of Mantua. He was in any case a more considerable artist than Balzac depicts in the character of Porbus, and Poussin in fact owed his own high style in part to Pourbus's example. In 1612, Pourbus was scarcely about to be surpassed in the Queen's artistic favor by Rubens, as Balzac suggests, though in 1621—the year before Pourbus's death—Rubens was to undertake the tremendous cycle of paintings which mythologized the life of Marie de Medici in the gallery of the Luxembourg Palace.

Frenhofer of course is entirely fictitious. But Balzac provides him with a real pedigree as the only student of Mabuse—the nickname of Jan Gossart, the Flemish painter who had died in 1532. Assuming Frenhofer had entered Mabuse's studio at the age of twelve, he would be ninety-two when the story takes place, but still a powerful painter and something of a lover as well. Artistic and erotic powers are crucially linked in Balzac's scheme. Porbus's waning powers are emblematized through the fact that, unlike either Poussin or Frenhofer, he lacks a female companion. He has only a female patron. In an atmosphere in which love and art are the main currencies, worldly power counts for very little.

The Unknown Masterpiece is an allegory of artistic glory and erotic love. The three painters are, so to speak, the spirits of Past, Present, and Future. For all the specifities of time and place, Balzac's story takes place in a poetical setting: "The dim light of the staircase lent a further tinge of the fantastic: as if a canvas by Rembrandt were walking, silent and unframed, through the tenebrous atmosphere that great painter had made his own."[4] In the successive versions of the story, which

---

4. In a kind of graphic footnote to *Le Chef-d'oeuvre inconnu*—Plate 36 of the so-called Vollard Suite of 1934—Picasso depicts what we may suppose is Frenhofer as Rembrandt. He showed the print to his mistress, Françoise,

Balzac revised over the course of more than fifteen years, the character of Frenhofer continues to deepen; by contrast, the two historical figures are frankly presented as stereotypes. Nicolas ("Nick" as the text playfully designates him) is the embodiment of the Bohemian Youth, the Young Man from the Provinces, poor enough that Frenhofer is moved to give him money to buy a good warm coat, and good-looking enough to be the lover of a "mistress of incomparable beauty—not one defect!" as Porbus will panderingly describe her to Frenhofer. Poussin's literary counterpart would have been Rodolphe in *Scènes de la vie de Bohème* by Balzac's friend Henri Murger (which was published a decade after the 1837 version of *Le Chef-d'oeuvre inconnu*). If Poussin is the Artist of the Future, Porbus embodies the Present in a wonderfully Balzacian way: an artist who has achieved

Gilot who lived with him in the rue des Grands-Augustins. Gilot recalls him saying, "You see this truculent character here, with the curly hair and moustache? That's Rembrandt. Or maybe Balzac; I'm not sure." Picasso was considerably older than Gilot, and very mindful of the disparity in age. What is striking is that Frenhofer-Rembrandt-Balzac-Picasso is evidently turned into a painting. He holds palette and brushes with one hand, and with the other he reaches out of the picture to hold hands with his young and achingly beautiful model. Artist and woman thus change places: in Balzac's story, the woman is in the picture and the artist is outside it; in Picasso's print, the painter is in the picture and the woman is outside. But they retain the kind of physical contact Frenhofer—and perhaps Balzac and Picasso—dreamt of. Though still a lover, Frenhofer may be too old for any more strenuous contact than holding hands, the way "Freno" in the film *La Belle noiseuse*—based on Balzac's story—lies chastely beside his mistress, holding hands, when the artistic-erotic renewal he had hoped for fails to materialize.

success in a style soon to be eclipsed by a shift in fashion to that of the Baroque—here embodied by Rubens, for whom Frenhofer expresses such contempt.

Frenhofer's role is to embody the Past, having learned the secrets of the masters. But in fact he is an anachronism, since Balzac depicts him in part as he would one of his own contemporaries. The remarkable passages in which Frenhofer repaints Porbus's picture of Marie Egyptienne disrobing in order to gain her passage to Jerusalem recapitulates what his biographers suggest was Balzac's own experience in sitting for Louis Boulanger's 1837 portrait of him. One chief difference between the first and the final recension of the story consists in Balzac having added a great deal of studio detail in depicting Frenhofer as a painter. These passages, according to one scholar, "Take up two fifths of the first part and over one fourth of the entire story ... the most important of them shows him correcting Porbus' painting according to his own principles." These changes, based presumably on Balzac's observations, are what give substance to what might otherwise be mere parable. And they illustrate how he uses his knowledge of reality as ballast for his imagination. In *Lost Illusions*, Balzac composed a portrait of a writer which so draws upon the detailed knowledge of royalties, proofs, advertising, plagiarism, and the kind of practical knowledge which only a writer of his day and age could have possessed that it is fact and fiction at once.

It is difficult to identify an actual artist from the 1830s whose painting exemplifies the maxims implied in Frenhofer's discourse. The great painters of the age would have been Ingres and Delacroix, whose *Liberty Leading the People* provided the main buzz in the Salon of 1831, when *The Unknown Masterpiece* was first published in the periodical *L'Artiste*. But the *philosophy* of painting would have been fairly standard for anyone who had internalized the Romantic image of an artist. It would have to have been someone who painted the way Victor Hugo wrote. We can get a pretty fair sense of the Frenhoferian spirit from the following passage by John Ruskin, a serious draftsman and the great disciple of Turner. Ruskin is describing an episode in which he drew an aspen near Fontainebleau in 1842:

> Languidly, but not idly, I began to draw it; and as I drew, the languor passed away. The beautiful lines insisted on being traced,—without weariness. More and more beautiful they became, as each rose out of the rest, and took its place in the air. With wonder increasing every instant, I saw that they "composed" themselves, by finer laws than any known of men. At last the tree was there, and everything I had thought before about trees, nowhere.

Notice the way the tree bodies itself forth "in the air." It is the "air" that makes the difference between

Frenhofer's work and Porbus's. "The air is so real you can no longer distinguish it from the air around yourselves," Frenhofer boasts. "There's no air between that arm and the background," he says in criticism of Porbus's figure. "You can see she's pasted on the canvas—you could never walk around her. She's a flat silhouette, a cutout who could never turn around or change position."[5]

Bringing reality to life has at once been the problem and promise of pictorial art. The history of painting as *problem* has in effect been a history of progress—the triumph over visual appearance, which is the overarching theme of Giorgio Vasari's great *Lives of the most Eminent Painters, Sculptors, and Architects*, first published in 1550; and more recently of Ernst Gombrich's *Art and Illusion*. For Vasari, as for Balzac's trinity of artists, that history culminates in Raphael. Thus Frenhofer removes his black velvet cap "to express his respect for this monarch of art." It is in any case a history of technical breakthroughs: perspective, chiaroscuro, foreshortening, anatomical understanding, physiognomy, optics,

---

5. The Realist painter, Gustav Courbet, is reported to have said, regarding the figure of Olympia in Manet's eponymous painting, "It's flat, it isn't modeled; it's like the Queen of Hearts after a bath." I had always taken this as a singular witticism, but Frenhofer's speech—written by Balzac nearly three decades before Manet's controversial work was painted—makes me believe that it must have been a standard put-down in studio crits at the time. Had Porbus not felt such great veneration for Frenhofer, he might have responded as Manet himself did: "Courbet bores us in the end with his modeling: his ideal is a billiard ball."

and color theory—the things that were taught in the academies, and which the real Poussin had to struggle so to master. When Frenhofer explains why his painting is such a triumph, his speech is like boilerplate from a painter's manual of the seventeenth century: "Some of these shadows cost me a lot of hard work.... I've managed to capture the truth of light and to combine it with the gleaming whiteness of the highlights, and ... by an opposite effort, by smoothing the ridges and textures of the paint itself and ... by submerging them in half-tones, have eliminated the very notion of drawing."

All of this could be taught and learned. But something else had entered the concept of art as early as the late eighteenth century, in the writing of Kant, namely, the concept of the creative genius: "a talent," Kant writes, "for producing that for which no definite rule can be given." Hence the genius "does not know himself how he has come by his ideas; and he has not the power to devise the like at pleasure, or in accordance with a plan, and to communicate it to others in precepts that will enable them to produce similar products." "Let's not analyze it," Frenhofer says. "It would only drive you to despair."

Frenhofer means that there are no rules. "It is not the mission of art to copy nature"—for which rules can be stated or mechanisms like the camera be devised—"but to express it!" And this then requires genius. Geniuses, Ruskin wrote, "are more instinctive and less reasonable than other people." He is referring to what happens when he, for example, draws a tree, and something beyond knowledge takes over: "I don't think myself a great genius—but I believe I have genius." Frenhofer puts it in his own way: "Artists aren't mere imitators, they're poets!" Somewhat inconsistently, Frenhofer appears to have imagined, in connection with the climactic work to which he devoted so many years, that knowledge really could do the work of genius—that knowledge, astutely applied, could not merely conquer appearance but conquer reality, and bring the subject literally to life. But Frenhofer, though unquestionably meant to be seen by us as a genius, aspires to something greater by far than that. He wants to perform magic.

This connects with the *promise* of pictorial art, which has a very different history from that of painterly progress. It is in effect a history of magic and of miracle. It is a history as well of superstition and of fear. In his brilliant study *Likeness and Presence*, the art historian Hans Belting has written an astonishing history of the devotional image in early Christian art. The early Church had no interest in pictures that were produced by the exercise of pictorial skills. It was rather interested in images that materialized without the intervention of an artist at all—the way the face of Jesus was miraculously imprinted on Veronica's veil, or Christ's tortured body on the Shroud of Turin. The Church worshiped Saint Luke's portrait of the Holy Virgin because it was believed that the Virgin herself magically formed her self-image on Luke's panel. There was no interest whatever in aesthetics or in artistic virtuosity. Images, when authentic, were like relics: the saint was believed to be embodied in his or her icons, and could be prayed to for benign interventions. We still hear about wonder-working Virgins and *Sacri Bambini*. These are images that have no reference to museums of fine art or to connoisseurship or art appreciation, nor do they belong in collections. Stories about them appear in the Metro sections of newspapers, but not in the sections devoted to culture.

From the perspective of magic, *every* image has the possibility of coming to life, and perhaps the first images ever drawn, however crudely executed, were viewed with an awe that still remains a disposition of the most primitive regions of the human brain. This is why images have been forbidden in so many of the great religions of the world, and why they have been destroyed in the name of iconoclasm. It is why Plato was afraid of art, and drove artists from his Republic. History and literature are filled with legends of images that come to life (think of the portrait of Dorian Gray). Mythical artists like "Master Pygmalion" have been envied and emulated by those with Frenhoferian ambitions. Pygmalion fulfilled the dream that artists can turn their effigies into real beings. By carving and polishing, his statue came to life! "You're in the presence of a woman. And you're still looking for a picture," Frenhofer tells his stupefied colleagues, who are unable to see either—who see only a "wall of paint." And we are left in the end wondering if the old painter has lost his mind or the younger painters have lost their eyes.

I want to respond to this in a moment, but I must first point out a third history, interwoven with the other two, as it is in Balzac's story. In this history, there are certain parallels between looking at a picture and looking at a woman—particularly at a woman's nakedness if one happens to be a man. There are traditions in which it is regarded as dangerous, or even lethal, for a man to see a woman's genital area. But that aura extends, in certain cultures, to all parts of a woman's body, which must be veiled to protect her from the gaze of males—and males from the sight of unveiled women! Balzac allows us to infer that in Frenhofer's painting, his mistress, Catherine Lescault—who is further described in all but the final version of the story as the courtesan known as *La Belle noiseuse*[6]—is depicted naked. The artist's extreme reluctance to allow anyone to look at his painting must mean that she is shown nude, so that seeing the

---

6. The name translates roughly into "The Beautiful Pain in the Ass." Intuitively, it sounds like someone's real nickname, and I could not help but feel that Catherine Lescault was a historical person. In the film *La Belle noiseuse*, the modern-day Frenhofer mentions a book about her. So far as I have been able to determine, however, she is entirely fictional, nickname and all. Richard Howard's translation follows Balzac's final version of *Le Chef-d'oeuvre inconnu* by omitting the name *La Belle noiseuse*.

picture is equivalent to seeing Catherine herself naked. Even in fairly recent memory, when nude photographs of the singer Madonna were printed in *Playboy*, it was at first felt that this must be an extreme embarrassment to her and, at the very least, an invasion of her privacy. There are real-life scenarios in which possessing nude photographs of a woman would give someone the power to blackmail her.

Frenhofer will finally permit his painting to be viewed only because this is the price he has to pay for being able to complete it. He evidently cannot complete it until he finds the right model: "I've made up my mind to travel—I'm off to Greece, to Turkey, even Asia, to look for a model." One wonders what has happened to the original model, Catherine Lescault herself. Perhaps she is no longer as beautiful as she once was, which is what happens to the model in Henry James's later story "The Madonna of the Future," in which the painter waits for too many years to execute his great painting.[7] In fact, I believe there is a more natural explanation, but in any case Porbus tells him that Poussin's mistress, Gillette, is of an incomparable beauty. And he tempts the old painter with an irresistible bargain: in exchange

---

7. James's story is sometimes said to be based on Balzac's. Since in none of the five essays he wrote on Balzac does he mention, let alone discuss, the *Chef-d'oeuvre inconnu*, one is almost obliged to believe that he was somehow suppressing the influence. At least certain current views of literary influence would say that Balzac's story must be what James's is about!

for allowing him to use Gillette as the needed model, he must permit Poussin and himself to see *La Belle noiseuse*. There is thus a symbolic exchange of women. Poussin and Porbus are allowed to see Catherine Lescault, in exchange for Frenhofer being allowed to see Gillette naked. Since Gillette is required to strip, we know that Catherine herself is naked in Frenhofer's painting, which explains why Frenhofer kept his painting of her veiled.

In terms of their values, both men have made an immense sacrifice for the sake of art. It is as if only something of a magic potency as great as that possessed by women (or at least by beautiful women) is sufficient to transfigure a picture into reality. Small wonder feminists have found reason to question the Male Gaze! Small wonder Gillette (as if posing for a canvas by Delacroix) "stood before him in the innocent posture of a terrified Circassian girl carried off by brigands to some slave dealer." How desperately Mary needed to be in Jerusalem, in the scene depicted by Porbus, can be measured by the fact that the boatman is given the inestimable privilege of seeing her bared breasts. Small wonder Frenhofer's main criticism of Porbus's picture is that "everything's wrong" in the way in which he painted Mary's bosom: the painting of the breasts should be as compelling as the breasts themselves.

From the story's perspective, of course, the gaze does not make objects of women, as feminist theory insists.

Rather, the story regards the bare female body as of so high a potency that it verges on numinousness. It is to be seen only by a man who occupies the position of the bridegroom. If it should be seen by anyone else, it loses its tremendous value entirely. The woman is cheapened beyond recovery. This is why modesty was once so exalted a feminine virtue. This is something Gillette completely understands. She has no choice but to hate her lover for having allowed this to happen: "Kill me! I'd be vile to love you still—you fill me with contempt."[8] Notice that we are still talking about visual perception: there is no question of Frenhofer having made love to Gillette, and, needless to say, no question of carnal congress between the two other artists and the *portrait* of Catherine Lescault! The symbolic equivalence the story establishes between seeing a woman's exposed body and seeing a work of art is an effort on the part of a Romantic writer to find something as valuable as art itself—something that money cannot buy, for a woman's nakedness is without value if it is bought. We get, in brief, a value scheme in which a kind of Taliban attitude toward female flesh is rendered equivalent to a Romantic's adoration of art as the supreme value of life.

The sequestration of women behind veils is of a piece with the hiddenness of art Walter Benjamin appeals to

8. When Fernande Olivier moved in with Picasso in 1905, he demanded that she stop modeling. He even sought to lock her up when he was away from the studio.

in order to account for art's aura. The publicity of the museum, in which everything is there to be looked at, is like the parade of women at the Folies Bergères, their nakedness stripped of its awesomeness. What makes Frenhofer so difficult for us to understand is that he fuses the mystery of female flesh with the magic of the work of art. But this fusion works only if it is a portrait of a woman the artist actually loves, whether or not it actually shows her naked. The story could hardly have worked had Frenhofer been painting fruit all that time like Cézanne! Given the intensity of the fused entity, it is hardly matter for amazement that the picture cannot live up to expectations. Of course the two other artists see, relative to what they have been led to expect, nothing. If all it is is a painting—a mere *painting*—well, it might just as well be what the mere human eye makes out: "a mass of strange lines forming a wall of paint" with an incongruously "living foot... [which] appeared there like the torso of some Parian Venus rising out of the ruins of a city burned to ashes."[9] If painting has lost

9. The celebrated "wall of paint"—*une muraille de peinture*—which Poussin sees instead of the "woman lying on a velvet coverlet, her bed surrounded by draperies, and at her side a golden tripod exhaling incense" he had expected from Frenhofer's exultant description of his masterpiece, was not a thinkable misadventure in seventeenth-century studio practice. "Paints were expensive in those days," Balzac correctly observes, even for an artist as rich as Frenhofer. Only in the twentieth century, with Monet's *Water Lilies* or the Abstract Expressionist canvases of Pollock or de Kooning, could a painting have been botched through that kind of material excess. In Balzac's day, artists' pigments were available in relatively inexpensive tubes, and this

its promise, artists have lost their power—so what's the point of art? And what's the point of going on painting if the best you can hope for is merely to make pictures?

That may be good enough for Poussin, who at the end of life could say, complacently, *"Je n'ai rien négligé"*—"I have neglected nothing." It had to be enough for Porbus, who was after all the favorite painter of a woman to whom he presumably would not have been united otherwise than as an external portraitist. It was not enough for Frenhofer, whose vision of art was as mystical as that of Balzac. It was not unless solving the problems of painting—which he had done—was the means to securing the mythic promise of painting, at which he necessarily failed: the transformation of a painted woman into a real one. In my view that failure explains why he burned all his paintings and then died. And it explains, I think, why Catherine Lescault was unavailable to him as a model. She was dead, and the only way she could be returned to life was through painting. He could not finish the painting since he could not re-create life. He saw what he had achieved as of a very different order of failure than what Poussin and Porbus saw. As an afterthought, one might conjecture that when it was widely seen that Frenhofer's failure was inescapable, due to an inherent limitation on realism, Modernism was ready to

made possible the direct approach to painting that Romanticism required. When Frenhofer complains about the pigments in Porbus's studio, he is speaking like someone who takes the art supply store as a given.

begin. Indeed, it is irresistible to see that wall of paint, crisscrossed with lines and with the realistic fragment of a woman's foot, as the first truly Modernist work!

But in what sense is *La Belle noiseuse*—which we may as well consider the work's title—a masterpiece? And in what sense is it unknown? It could not have been known, in 1612, as a Modernist masterpiece. The concept did not exist. Neither, for that matter, did the concept of Mannerism exist. Both of these were stylistic terms, devised by art historians in the twentieth century, to designate bodies of work with certain affinities to one another. Modernism is sometimes thought to have begun with Manet, and Manet is a good case to consider here, since his work was radically misperceived in its time, and his masterpiece, *Déjeuner sur l'herbe*, relegated to the Salon des refusés, where it was jeered at by an outraged public. It was an "unknown masterpiece" in the sense that, though a masterpiece, few at the time would have recognized it as such. Ruskin wrote: "I am fond of standing by a bright Turner in the Academy, to listen to the unintentional compliments of the crowd—'What a glaring thing!' 'I declare I can't look at it!' 'Don't it hurt your eyes!' " I myself once overheard someone scoffing at the Turners in the Tate, saying, "Whoever told him he could paint?" Turner's works are still not seen by everyone as the masterpieces they are. In the context of Balzac's story, the term *inconnu* means "unrecognized."

It might seem difficult to suppose that painters as gifted as Poussin and Porbus could fail to recognize a masterpiece when they see one, but that is the story of art. In 1612, Poussin's paradigm was the School of Fontainebleau. For Pourbus, Titian set the criterion for painterly excellence. Imagine that they had been presented with one of Cézanne's masterpieces, or de Kooning's *Woman I*, or Pollock's *Blue Poles*. Nothing in their experience would have prepared them to see these as art at all. They would have looked to them like ruined canvas, smeared over by a madman or an animal. Frenhofer himself could hardly have recognized *La Belle noiseuse* as a masterpiece. We would want to reverse his speech, saying to him, "You're in the presence of a painting. But you're still looking for a woman." It would have been of no interest to him whatever to learn that he was ahead of his time, "The First Modernist." He is not interested in art history. He is interested in the power of images to come to life. Even if it is a great painting, it has, from the perspective of magic, to be a bleak failure.

Under the auspices of Balzac's Romanticism, a great work of art was equivalent in value to the body of a beloved woman. And if no one could see its greatness, that is what one must expect. Greatness in art is disclosed in time, as the body of the woman is revealed to the rightful eye of love.

John Updike on

SEVEN MEN

BY MAX BEERBOHM

THE MATHEMATICALLY adept reader, counting the names of the men named in the table of contents of *Seven Men*, will notice that there are only six. The seventh is the author, Max Beerbohm himself, who from story to story is seen interacting with his half-dozen heroes; in his elegant fashion he was as specialized and fantastical a specimen of late Imperial English manhood as any of these fictional creations. Born in 1872, he early developed a preternatural poise and grace as a writer and a caricaturist. While still an undergraduate at Oxford he became a contributor to *The Yellow Book*; Oxford became the magical milieu of his only novel, the blithe love-farce *Zuleika Dobson*, an extravagant collegiate *hommage*. Beerbohm retained into old age an undergraduate playfulness, spending much of his later years ornamenting with illustration, collage, and marginalia his own books and the books of others.

His life was bookish, but the bookishness was sunny, skimming the essence, in marvelous parodies, from his more earnest and ponderous contemporaries, and penning essays collected in volumes whose titles themselves signal a refusal to take his enterprise altogether seriously: the first was *The Works of Max Beerbohm*, followed by *More, Yet Again*, and *Even Now*. As a young man he cut a dandyish figure about London; George Bernard Shaw, whom he replaced as theater critic of *The Saturday Review* in 1898, dubbed him "the incomparable Max." In 1910 the maturing dandy married Florence Kahn, an American actress renowned for her portrayals of Ibsen heroines, and the couple took up residence, interrupted only by the two world wars, in Rapallo on the Italian Riviera. Keenly appreciated but not widely bought during his prime, he achieved geriatric celebrity with his reminiscing broadcasts over the BBC, beginning in 1935, and with the postwar biographical attentions of J. M. Rewald and S. N. Behrman. By his death in 1956, at the age of eighty-four, he seemed a carefully self-preserved souvenir of a spatted, strawhatted era long absorbed into history.

Always, even when in the thick of London literary life, Beerbohm projected the somewhat isolating aura of a man dancing to his own tune, who would not be deflected from his private bent by the competitive examples of others. The willful exquisitism of Wilde and Beardsley stayed with him after these hothouse flowers had met their dooms, taking the French perfumes of *fin de siècle* decadence with them; the heartily prolific late Victorians and Edwardians who were his contemporaries —Shaw, Wells, Chesterton, Belloc, Bennett, Galsworthy—

inspired him not to energetic emulation but to the scrupulous, devastating imitations collected in *A Christmas Garland*, the finest book of prose parodies in the English language. His brief preface arrestingly states an educational fact true for generations of British stylists:

> I had had some sort of aptitude for Latin prose and Latin verse. I wondered often whether those two things, essential though they were (and are) to the making of a decent style in English prose, sufficed for the making of a style more than decent. I felt that I must have other models. And thus I acquired the habit of aping, now and again, quite sedulously, this or that live writer—sometimes, it must be admitted, in the hope of learning rather what to avoid.

Henry James and Conrad earned, it would seem, his warmest admiration, and only Kipling, with his sometimes brutal jingoism, a real animosity. But the ambition of these men, their willingness to extend their gifts into laughable exertions, was alien to the incomparable Max. In "James Pethel," the most earnest of the stories collected in *Seven Men*, the somewhat Conradian hero says to the narrator, who has been admiring Pethel's nerve and sang-froid while gambling, "Ah, but you despise us all the same!" Us—the gamblers, the doers of the world. Pethel adds "that he has always envied men who had resources within themselves." Beerbohm, by his account, in answer "laughed lightly, to imply that it was very pleasant to have such resources, but that I didn't want to boast." A few pages later in the evening of this encounter, Pethel, who has described himself as a "very great admirer" of Beerbohm's work,

> asked what I was writing now, and said that he looked to me to "do something big, one of these days," and that he was sure I had it "in" me. This remark (though of course I pretended to be pleased by it) irritated me very much.

The story that contains this delicately confessional exchange is the only one that has no element of formal parody and that shows, in driving home its moral, some strain: Beerbohm's antipathy to ruthless gamblers exceeds, by a shade, the reader's.

Pethel, with no interior artistic resources, must keep testing himself, and those he loves, against high-stakes risk; the heroes of the other four tales are captive to imaginations more distinctly literary. A.V. Laider's "limpness of demeanor" is marked only by an incongruous shock of white hair that gives him a touch of the charlatan; behind his bland reticence he is revealed to be a compulsive story-spinner, a wildly inventive bard. The tortuous shifts and obsessive pains of literary rivalry are displayed with a fiendish animation in "Hilary

Maltby and Stephen Braxton," a distinguished specimen of the raft of ghost stories which Victorian religiosity trailed after it. The moment when poor Maltby is, while attending church service, encased within the phantom body of his rival—"All I knew was a sudden black blotting-out of things; an infinite and impenetrable darkness. . . . I calculate that as we sat there my eyes were just beneath the roof of his mouth. Horrible!"—transcends comedy, funny as it is, and touches a chord worthy of an earthier author, deep within the human body, where Beerbohm did not usually choose to go.

Maltby's nightmare, given a placid dénouement in Italy's Lucca, and "'Savonarola' Brown" both date from 1917, when Beerbohm, having taken shelter from the First World War in a cottage on the English farm of his friend the painter Will Rothenstein, found further shelter in recollection of the literary London of his youth. Brown, first met at school and remet fifteen years later, is a "second-nighter"—a more passionate devotee of the stage than the showy first-nighters. "He did not seem to know much, or to wish to know more, about life. Books and plays, first editions and second nights, were what he cared for." The model tragedy, concerning the Florentine monk Savonarola, upon which Brown has been portentously laboring, turns out, when he dies, to be one act short of five, and in its maladroit blank verse and mob of Renaissance characters a travesty of Shakespeare. Max was a versifier of dainty skill, and the comic effects, to be savored line by line, hinge on fine points, such as contractions run riot to fit the meter, unhappy coinages like "friskfulness," clanging iambs, and drooping enjambments. Yet there is something wild and disheveled about the piece overall, especially the last three pages, where Beerbohm asserts his own presence; Bardolatry is possibly so big and well-armored that it has splayed his pen.

"Enoch Soames" is the first and oldest of these sketches, and to me the most moving. The littérateur who has everything—dedication, ego, bohemian flair, an adequate private income—except talent is an apparition too close to home for any writer to contemplate without unease. The narrator's tone, especially intimate and insistent, urges our sober attention, yet with a lovely urbane lightness carries off even the shopworn presence of the Devil, in a fondly described vanished restaurant. Soames's visit, purchased at the price of his soul, to the British Museum of a hundred years hence is heartbreaking—a visit to his own nonexistence, in the one realm that matters to him.

Were Beerbohm, now, to make a similar pilgrimage, he would be greeted by more structural changes, in the grand but overburdened research facility, than his tale predicts, but he would be rewarded by finding in the fabled catalog (computer-accessed by now) not only his modest list of titles but enough bibliographical

attention to flatter a major artist. Minor artistry became in him a creed, a boast; like Ronald Firbank and
Nathanael West, he remains readable while many might-
ier *oeuvres* gather dust. The filigree is fine, but of the
purest gold.

Jonathan Lethem on

ON THE YARD

BY MALCOLM BRALY

THE MIND flinches from the fact of prisons—their prevalence, squatting in the midst of towns and cities, their role in so many lives, and in the history and everyday life of our country. And when the mind does find its way there, it wants the whole subject covered in hysteria and overstatement. Let prisons be one simple thing —either horrific zoos for the irretrievably demented and corrupt, or inhumane machines which grind down innocent men. Let them stand apart as raw cartoons of black-and-white morality, having nothing to do with the rest of us—we who live in the modulated, ambivalent, civilized world "the novel" was born to depict. We might secretly feel prison doesn't *need* a novel, that it instead needs a miniseries or the Op-Ed page.

Malcolm Braly's *On the Yard*, temperate and unhysterical as its title, is the novel prison needs. It's also a book any lover of novels ought to know, for its compression, surprise, and wry humor, for its deceptively casual architecture, and for characters and scenes which are unforgettable. Of course, readers may be compelled to read realistic novels set in war or plague or prison by uneasy cravings to know particulars of lives they hope never to encounter more directly. And Braly surely has knowledge we don't, tons of it. During a miserable, nearly fatherless childhood, Braly began acting out his grievances through a series of petty and eventually not-so-petty burglaries, until, in the company of some reckless partners in crime, he found himself in an interstate chase which climaxed in a gun battle with police, then capture and imprisonment. Upon his first release he slipped back into a desultory pattern of minor crime; eventually managing to spend a majority of his first forty years of life behind prison walls without having murdered or raped, without having even stolen anything of much value.

Apart from knowledge, Braly possesses an insouciant tone of confidence which causes us never to doubt him, and which is more persuasive than any fact: if these things can be taken as givens, taken almost lightly, then truly the prison is another world as real as our own. But beyond reportage, or tourism, *On the Yard* succeeds because through its particulars it becomes universal, a model for understanding aspects of our self-wardened lives. Inside and outside prison walls human beings negotiate, stall, bluff, and occasionally explode in their attempts to balance ecstasy against ennui, to do more than merely eke out their narrowing days on earth. But Braly skirts allegory: his book is much too lean and local to bother with that. The reader supplies the allegory.

The novel could be said to center on the plateau and fall (we never witness his rise) of Chilly Willy, a prison racketeer who deftly controls a small empire of cigarettes, pharmaceutical narcotics, and petty bureaucratic favors, orchestrated by a routine of minimal violence and, as his name suggests, maximum cool. Despite his name, and the outlines of his career, he's a deeply real and human character, even a sympathetic one. We watch as Chilly manipulates the razor's-edge power dynamics of the prison until a single miscalculation causes him to lash out. It is then that the prison administration undertakes Chilly's destruction, by the simple act of placing a receptively homosexual cellmate in his previously solitary cell. The new cellmate serves as Chilly's mirror—not for a repressed homosexuality, but for the fact that his manipulations had always had concealed within them a grain of solicitude, perhaps even disguised family feeling. The men Chilly commands are under his care, however apparently dispassionate a form this care has taken. Sex becomes the means of Chilly's self-destruction—but then nearly every character in the book is shown in a second act of self-destruction inside the prison, which recapitulates and confirms an initial act outside.

The novel *could* be said to center on Chilly's fall, except it barely centers anywhere, moving by its own cool strategy through the minds and moments of dozens of characters, some recurrently, some only for a sole brief visitation which nearly always proves definitive. Three or four of these are into the minds of the prison's keepers, including that of the morose, long-enduring Warden. The rest are a broad array of prisoners, some "hardened" repeaters, some newly arrived at San Quentin, some floating in between and trying to measure the rightness and permanence of their placement inside those walls. All but the craziest and most loathsome—like the shoe-sniffing, anal-compulsive Sanitary Slim—are presented at least briefly as potential audience and author surrogates. All of them are rejected, either gently or rudely, by the end.

This is Braly's brilliantly successful game—he's a master at exploiting the reader's urge to identify with his characters. The results are estranging, in the best sense: both funny and profound. Each character undergoes a sort of audition. The first pair of candidates is offered in Chapter One: Nunn, a repeat offender shuffling his way back inside and trying to come to terms with his propensity for self-defeat, his missed opportunities during his brief stint outside, and Manning, a sensitive and observant first-timer who has overturned his innocuous life with a sudden and incomprehensible crime of sexual perversion. The reader begins to squirm in a way which will become familiar—ordinary guilt and innocence will not be our map here. Braly is enormously conscious of the effect of withholding the criminal histories of certain of his characters, while blurting others.

His writerly pleasure in this game is tipped in comic miniatures like this one: "He lit his cigarette, then held the match for Zekekowski, noting again how finely formed Zekekowski's hands were, actually beautiful, the hands of a . . . of an arsonist, as it happened."

If the men glimpsed in Braly's San Quentin break into roughly two groups, Manning and Nunn are typical of each: those who are career criminals, and those who have committed single crimes of impulse—the molesters and wife-killers. Braly leads us gently to the irony that the former commit relatively harmless crimes and yet are compulsively recurrent, whereas the latter are morally abhorrent yet less likely to return to the prison after their release. The impulsives are frequently bookish and bourgeois, unlike the careerists in outlook or temperament, and with a tendency to look down on them as lessers. At the extreme we meet Watson, a priggish impulsive: "Watson stood with culture, the Republic, and Motherhood. . . . He had killed his two small sons, attempted to kill his wife, . . . all because his wife had refused a reconciliation with the remark, 'John, the truth is you bore me.' " Watson defends himself in a therapy session, claiming, "I see no point in further imprisonment, further therapy, no point whatsoever since there's absolutely no possibility I'll do the same thing again." And he's immediately teased by the raffish, Popeye-like career criminal Society Red, who says, "That's right. . . . He's run out of kids."

More sympathetic is Lorin, a fragile jailhouse poet who cringes inside fantasies of Kim Novak and notebook jottings like *"Yet I am free—free as any to test the limits of my angry nerves and press the inner pains of my nature against the bruise of time."* Braly doesn't hold such sensitivity up for either mockery or admiration: like other responses to the condition known as San Quentin, it is simply presented as one possibility among many. Nearer to the author's own sympathies—or so a reader may suspect—is Paul Juleson, Lorin's sometime mentor and protector. Juleson at first glance seems the most resourceful and best equipped of the prison intellectuals, and therefore both a likely survivor and a good bet for author's proxy. In a flashback we learn that he killed his wife; the hell of his short marriage is portrayed with devastating economy and insight, and the violence of his crime doesn't impede our inclining toward Juleson's sympathies. Richard Rhodes, in *The New York Times*'s original review of *On the Yard*, came out and said it: "Juleson is probably Mr. Braly's alter ego." Yet I don't think it's so simple as that—and certainly Braly denies us the usual satisfactions of rooting for this character when, despite all his wiles and wisdom, Juleson puts himself in the path of Chilly Willy's contempt by a dumb play for a few packs of cigarettes.

From that point Chilly and Juleson catalyze one another's destruction. It is as though each man has been fated to expose the weakness in the other. So if Braly has an alter ego in the book, it is split, in an act of symbolic self-loathing, between these two men. Rhodes, in his otherwise admiring review, went on to call the book "curiously ambivalent, as though the author had not yet sorted out his own attitudes when he wrote it." I think this ambivalence, far from unintentional, is in fact the essence of Braly's art. The criminal professionals are not so different from the middle-class murderers after all— they are united in self-destruction. San Quentin exists, at some level, because these men need a place to solve the puzzle of their lives by nullification. It also exists because of our society's need to accommodate that nullification, giving it four square walls, a pair of coveralls, and a number, as well as a few perfunctory hours of group therapy a week.

In other words, if it's difficult to discern with whom Malcolm Braly identifies, this is likely because Malcolm Braly doesn't identify with himself. Not exactly. This becomes plain in Braly's *False Starts*, his extraordinary memoir of his childhood, and of his pathetic criminal and prison careers. In this second masterpiece, published ten years after *On the Yard*, Braly marvels extensively at his own tropism for the prison, at those miraculous self-sabotages which led him again and again to the miserable comforts of incarceration. We learn that during one break-in he actually managed to accidentally leave behind a slip of paper bearing his full name and address, as though desperate to devise a path back inside.

Standing outside *On the Yard*'s character scheme is the lanky teenage sociopath, Stick. Leader of a mostly imaginary gang of fascist hoodlums called The Vampires, Stick is a cipher of human chaos, and he eventually brings down an unlikely destruction on the prison. Stick's uncanny near-escape is by hot-air balloon, one painstakingly constructed by his cellmate and stolen by Stick at the last moment. This reveals a vein of dreamy masturbatory fantasy, a childishness, which our fear of criminals and prisoners usually conceals from us, but which Braly doesn't want concealed. The balloon is an unusually direct symbol for any novel, but especially Braly's. Nonetheless, it bears evidence of that ambivalence which marks all the characters and their strivings: when examiners consider the crashed balloon they find it scored by excessively reworked sewing, which has weakened the fabric: "[the stitches] suggested an analogy to hesitation marks in a suicide." Stick also, it seems to me, reveals *On the Yard* as being a 1960s California book, and San Quentin in the Sixties as being oddly subject to the same propensity for utopianism and social experiment as the Bay Area within which the prison darkly huddles. In an eastern prison Stick might more likely have been drawn into some preexisting gang or mafia: thirty years later he'd be a Crip or Blood. Here he's free to self-invent, and so becomes a prognostication of Charles Manson or Jim Jones.

Malcolm Braly's life was sad, triumphant, and sad

again. He lived mostly inside for twenty years, until his writing, together with the will and generosity of Gold Medal Books editor Knox Burger, provided a rescue. He died in a car accident at fifty-four, leaving behind a wife and infant daughter—Knox Burger has said he was "fat and happy." His peak as a writer came in the two complementary books, the novel and the memoir, and in the memoir he says about the novel, "I was writing over my head." A reader needn't explore the earlier books to confirm this, for Braly is working over his head in *On the Yard* in the sense that any novelist is when he has moved beyond his tools, or through them, to experience a kind of transubstantiation with his characters. At those moments a writer always knows more than he ever could have expected to, and he can only regard the results with a kind of honest awe. The book is no longer his own, but a vehicle by which anyone can see himself both exculpated and accused, can find himself alternately imprisoned and freed. Braly's novel is something like Stick's borrowed balloon, in the end, a beautiful, unlikely oddment rising from the yard of San Quentin, motley with the scars of its making and no less perfect for showing those "hesitation marks." It rises above the prison walls in a brief, glorious flight, before gravity makes its ordinary claim.

Toni Morrison on

THE RADIANCE OF THE KING
BY CAMARA LAYE

OF THE velvet-lined offering plates passed down the pews on Sunday, the last one was the smallest and the most empty. Its position and size signaled the dutiful but limited expectations that characterized most everything in the Thirties. The coins, never bills, sprinkled there were mostly from children encouraged to give up their pennies and nickels for the charitable work so necessary for the redemption of Africa. Such a beautiful word, Africa. Unfortunately its seductive sound was riven by the complicated emotions with which the name was associated. Unlike starving China, Africa was both ours and theirs; us and other. A huge needy homeland none of us had seen or cared to see, inhabited by people with whom we maintained a delicate relationship of mutual ignorance and disdain, and with whom we shared a mythology of passive, traumatized otherness cultivated by textbooks, films, cartoons, and the hostile name-calling children learn to love.

World War II was over before I sampled fiction set in Africa. Often brilliant, always compelling, these narratives elaborated on the very mythology that accompanied

those velvet plates floating between the pews. For Joyce
Cary, Elspeth Huxley, H. Rider Haggard, Africa was
precisely what the missionary collection implied: a dark
continent in desperate need of light. The light of Christianity, of civilization, of development. The light of
charity switched on by simple human pity. It was an
idea of Africa fraught with the assumptions of a complex intimacy coupled with an acknowledgment of profound estrangement. This combination of ownership
and strangeness unfettered the imagination of fiction
writers and, just as it had historians and explorers, en-
ticed them into projecting a metaphysically void Africa
ripe for invention.

Literary Africa—outside, notably, of the work of some
white South African writers—was an inexhaustible
playground for tourists and foreigners. In the novels
and stories of Joseph Conrad, Isak Dinesen, Saul Bellow,
Ernest Hemingway, whether imbued with or struggling
against conventional Western views of benighted Africa,
their protagonists found the continent to be as empty
as the collection plate—a vessel waiting for whatever
copper and silver imagination was pleased to place
there. Accommodatingly mute, conveniently blank,
Africa could be made to serve a wide variety of literary
and/or ideological requirements: it could stand back
as scenery for any exploit, or leap forward and obsess
itself with the woes of any foreigner; it could contort
itself into frightening malignant shapes in which West-

erners could contemplate evil, or it could kneel and accept elementary lessons from its betters. For those who made either the literal or the imaginative voyage, contact with Africa, its penetration, offered thrilling opportunities to experience life in its primitive, formative, inchoate state, the consequence of which experience was knowledge—a wisdom that confirmed the benefits of European proprietorship and, more importantly, enabled a self-revelation free of the responsibility of gathering overly much actual intelligence about the African cultures. So big-hearted was this literary Africa, its invitation to explore the inner life was never burdened by an impolite demand for reciprocal generosity. A little geography, lots of climate, a few customs and anecdotes became the canvas upon which a portrait of a wiser or sadder or fully reconciled self could be painted.

In Western novels published up to and throughout the 1950s, Africa, while offering the occasion for knowledge, seemed to keep its own unknowableness intact. Very much like Charlie Marlowe's "white patch for a boy to dream over." Mapped since his boyhood with "rivers and lakes and names, [it] had ceased to be a blank space of delightful mystery . . . It had become a place of darkness." What little could be known was enigmatic, repugnant, or hopelessly contradictory. Imaginary Africa was a cornucopia of imponderables that resisted explanation; riddles that defied solution; conflicts that not only did not need to be resolved, but needed to exist if the process of self-discovery was to have the widest range of play. Thus the literature resounded with the clash of metaphors. As the original locus of the human race, Africa was ancient; yet, being under colonial control, it was also infantile. Thus it became a kind of old fetus always waiting to be born but confounding all midwives. In novel after novel, short story after short story, Africa was simultaneously innocent and corrupting, savage and pure, irrational and wise. It was raw matter out of which the writer was free to forge a template to examine desire and improve character. But what Africa never was, was its own subject, as America has been for European writers, or England, France, or Spain for their American counterparts.

Even when Africa was ostensibly a subject, its people were oddly dehumanized in ways both pejorative and admiring. In Isak Dinesen's recollections the stock of similes she draws on most frequently to describe the inhabitants belongs to the animal world. "The old dark clear-eyed native of Africa, and the old dark clear-eyed elephant—they are alike." The "hind part of a little old woman ... is like a picture of an ostrich." Groups of men are "herd[s] of sheep," "old mules." Masai finery is "stags' antlers." And in a moment meant to register the poignant heartache of leaving Africa, Dinesen writes of a woman as follows: "When we met she stood dead still, barring the path to me, staring at me in the exact manner of a Giraffe in a herd, that you will meet on the open plain, and which lives and feels and thinks in a manner unknowable to us. After a moment she broke out weeping, tears streaming over her face, like a cow that makes water on the plain before you."

In that racially charged context, being introduced in the early Sixties to the novels of Chinua Achebe, the work of Wole Soyinka, Ama Ata Aidoo, and Cyprian Ekwenski, to name a few, was more than a revelation— it was intellectually and aesthetically transforming. But coming upon Camara Laye's *Le Regard du roi* in the English translation known as *The Radiance of the King* was shocking. This extraordinary novel accomplished something brand new. The clichéd journey into African darkness either to bring light or to find it is reimagined here. In fresh metaphorical and symbolical language, storybook Africa, as site of therapeutic exploits or of sentimental initiations leading toward life's diploma, is reinvented. Employing the idiom of the conqueror, using exactly and precisely the terminology of the dominant discourse on Africa, this extraordinary Guinean author plucked at the Western eye to prepare it to meet the "regard," the "look," the "gaze" of an African king.

If one is writing within and about an already "raced" milieu, advocacy and argument are irresistible. Rage against the soul murder embedded in the subject matter runs the risk of destabilizing the text, forcing the "raced" writer to choose among a limited array of strategies: documenting the seethe; conscientiously, studiously avoiding it, struggling to control it; pretending it does not exist, or, as in this instance, manipulating its heat. Animating its dross into a fine art of subversive potency. Like a blacksmith transforming a red-hot lump of iron into a worthy blade, Camara Laye exchanged African "enigma" and darkness for subtlety, for literary ambiguity. Eschewing argument by assertion, he claimed the right to intricacy, to nuance, to insinuation—claims which may have contributed to a persistent interpretation of the novel either as a simple race-inflected allegory or as dream-besotted mysticism.

Camara Laye not only summoned a sophisticated, wholly African imagistic vocabulary in which to launch a discursive negotiation with the West, he exploited with technical finesse the very images that have served white writers for generations. The filthy inn where Clarence, the protagonist, is living could be taken word for word from Joyce Cary's *Mister Johnson*; his susceptibility to and obsession with smells read like a play upon Elspeth Huxley's *The Flame Trees of Thika*; his European fixation with the "meaning" of nakedness recalls H. Rider Haggard or Joseph Conrad or virtually all travel writing. Reworking the hobbled idioms of imperialism, colonialism, and racism, Camara Laye allows us the novel experience of both being and watching an anonymous interloper discover not a new version of himself via a country waiting for Western imagination to bring it into view, but an Africa already idea-ed, gazing upon the other.

Clarence, a European, disembarks in an unnamed African country as an adventurer, one gathers. It is not made clear what compels this journey. He is not on a mission, or a game hunt, nor does he claim to be exhausted by the pressures of Western civilization. Yet his desire to penetrate Africa is urgent enough to risk drowning. "Twenty times" the tide carries his boat toward and away from the shore. Quite deliberately and significantly, Camara Laye spends no time describing Clarence's past or his motives for traveling to Africa. He can forgo with confidence a novelist's obligation to provide background material and rely on the conventions of white-man-in-Africa narratives wherein the reason for the quest is itself a prickly question since it often involves less than innocent impulses. In Saul Bellow's *Henderson the Rain King* one chapter opens, "What made me take this trip to Africa? There is no quick explanation"; and another, "And now a few words about my reasons for going to Africa." The answer, forthrightly, is desire: "I want. I want. I want."

Conrad's characters are driven to Africa by passionate curiosity or else assigned, as it were. One way or another we are to believe they have as little choice to make the trip as the indigenous people have to receive them. Hemingway, even as he experiences the continent (empty except for game and servants) as his private preserve, allows his characters to imply the question and hazard emotional answers. "Africa was where Harry had been happiest in the good times of his life, so he had come out here to start again." "Africa cleans out your liver," Robert Wilson tells Francis Macomber, "burns fat from the soul." Clarence, too, posits the question repeatedly. " 'Why did I want to cross that reef at all costs?' he wondered. 'Could I not have stayed where I was?' But stay where? . . . on the boat? Boats are only transitory dwellings! . . . 'I might have thrown myself overboard,' he thought. But wasn't that exactly what he had done? " " 'Can that [life beyond death] be the sort of life I have come here to find?' " Whatever the answer, we never expect what Camara Laye offers: an Africa answering back.

Clarence's immediate circumstance is that he has gambled, lost, and, heavily in debt to his white compatriots, is hiding among the indigenous population in a dirty inn. Already evicted from the colonists' hotel, about to be evicted by the African innkeeper, Clarence's solution to his penilessness (with the habitual gambler's insouciance) is to be taken into "the service of the king." He has no skills or qualities for the job, but he has one asset that always works, can only work, in third world countries. He is white, he says, and therefore suited in some ineffable way to be adviser to a king he has never seen, in a country he does not know, among people he neither understands nor wishes to.

His sense of entitlement, however, is muted by timidity and absence of esteem, "having lost the right—the right or the luxury—to be angry." He is prevented by a solid crowd of villagers from speaking to the king, but after a glimpse of him from afar, he is resolute. He meets a pair of mischief-loving teenagers and a cunning beggar who agree to help him out of his difficulty with the innkeeper and the surreal trial that follows. Under their hand-holding guidance he travels south where the king is expected to appear next. What begins as a quest for paid employment, for escape from the contempt of his white countrymen and unfair imprisonment in an African jail, could easily have become a novel about another desperate Westerner's attempt to reinvent himself. But Camara Laye's project is different: to investigate cultural perception and the manner in which knowledge arrives. The episodes Clarence confronts trace and parody the parallel sensibilities of Europe and Africa. Notions of status, civitas, custom, commerce, and intelligence; of law or of law versus morality—all are engaged here in nuanced dialogue; in scenes of raucous misunderstandings; in resonant encounters with "mythic" Africa.

Challenging the cliché of Africa as sensual/irrational, Camara Laye uses an "inferno of the senses" as a direct route to rationality. What Clarence sees first as dancers "freely improvis[ing], each without paying any attention to his companions," doing what he believes are "war dances," a "barbaric spectacle," turns out to be a group performing an intricate choreography of a star surrounding the king. Village huts that appear to him originally as monotonous, slipshod hovels he sees later as "magnificent pottery . . . the walls . . . smooth and sonorous as drums or deep bells, delicately, delightfully varnished and patinated, with the good smell of warm brick. . . . Windows like portholes had been let into the walls, just big enough to frame a face, yet not so big that any passing stranger could cast more than a swift glance into the interior of the hut. . . . Everything was perfectly clean: the roofs were newly thatched, the pottery shone as if it had been freshly polished." He hears indigenous music as "utterly without meaning"; "queer haphazard noise." In the forest that he finds "absolutely still," "completely empty," his companions hear drums announcing not just their arrival, but who, specifically, is arriving. The overpowering, repugnant "odor of warm wool and oil, a herdlike odor," becomes "a subtle combination of flower-perfumes and the exhalations of vegetable molds . . . a sweetish, heady, and disturbing odor . . . all-enveloping rather than repellent . . . caressing . . . alluring," and, one might add, addictive. He is touched, fondled, and spends his nights steeped in carnal pleasures. The author orchestrates the senses as conduits to available information and intelligence.

Principally, however, the novel focuses its attention on the authority of the gaze. Sight, blindness, shadows, myopia, astigmatism, delusion are the narrative figurations which lead Clarence and reader to the novel's dazzling epiphany. Ignorance and lack of insight are signaled by melting horizons, shifting architecture, torpor. People and events require constant revision. Although it is Clarence's wish for oblivion, to "sleep until the day of deliverance," until he can "catch the king's eye," information is all around him if he chooses to gather it. But Clarence looks away from faces, eyes. His habit of staring at the beggar's Adam's apple rather than his eyes costs him dearly. When, finally, he does look, "he thought he saw in them a dishonest look, a kind of irony, too, and perhaps both of these. . . . Something sly, insidious ? . . . Something faintly mocking? How could one tell?" When women appear he sees only their "luxuriant buttocks and breasts." Even the African woman he lives with is "no different from the others":

Akissi would put her face in the porthole's oval frame, and Clarence would be able to recognize it as hers. But as soon as he saw her whole body, it was as if he could no longer see her face: all he had eyes for were her buttocks and her breasts— the same high, firm buttocks and the same pear-shaped breasts as the other women. . . .

When Clarence is enslaved, he refuses to understand the negotiations for his bondage even though they take place in his presence. In his estimation, the conversations following the beggar's proposal to sell him are merely trivial or simply opaque; all subsequent hints of his services he dismisses as babble. When the "mystery" becomes so blatant that perception is inescapable he greets the inevitable with unease and lame, truncated questions minus genuine curiosity. Even as he gains rank in the village—now that he is of use—and pointed comments mount, he hides behind innocence. "Felt all over like a chicken on market-day" by the obese eunuch, Samba Baloum, Clarence is merely offended by the familiarity, unaware of the deal that has been struck. Because African laughter is senseless to him, he never gets the joke or recognizes double entendre. Dreams loaded with valuable information he finds "silly." Frequently disguised as dream, disorientation, or confusion, events and encounters designed to invite perception accumulate as Clarence's Western eye gradually undergoes transformation. "Clarence was now perfectly aware that he had been dreaming; but he could also see now that his dream was true."

What counts as intelligence here is the ability and willingness to see, surmise, understand. Clarence's confusion is deeply confusing to those around him. His refusal to analyze or meditate cogently on any event except the ones that concern his comfort or survival dooms him. When knowledge finally seeps through, he feels "annihilated" by it. Stripped of the hope of interpreting Africa to Africans and deprived of the responsibility of translating Africa to Westerners, Clarence provides us with an unprecedented sight: a male European, de-raced and de-cultured, experiencing Africa without resources, authority, or command. Because it is he who is marginal, ignored, superfluous; he whose name is never uttered until he is "owned"; he who is without history or representation; he who is sold and exploited for the benefit of a presiding family, a shrewd entrepreneur, a local regime; we observe an African culture being its own subject, initiating its own commentary.

Clarence does indeed find "the life which lies beyond death," but not before a reeducation process much like Camara Laye's own cultural education in Paris. Born on the first day of 1928 to an ancient Malinke family in Guinea, Camara Laye attended a Koranic school, a government school, and a technical college in Conakry. Awarded a scholarship at the age of nineteen, he left for France in 1947 to study automobile engineering. Memories of the solitude, poverty, and menial labor that were his lot in Paris became the genesis of his first book, the autobiographical *L'Enfant noir* (1953), praised and prized in France. Deep admiration for French art and culture did not rival his fervent love of his own. He entered the political climate of postcolonial Guinea and the strife-ridden relationship between France and francophone West Africa with the conviction that "the man of letters should contribute his writing to the revolution." His

proud commitment to this blend of art and politics, freedom and responsibility, had serious and damaging consequences: imprisonment by Sékou Touré, exile under
the protection of Léopold Senghor in Senegal, and a con-
stantly imperiled existence. Notwithstanding the usual
menu of cultural/educational/government posts offered
to writers, the trials of exile, and debilitating bouts of
illness, Camara Laye lectured, wrote plays, journalism,
and, in 1966, twelve years after the publication of *Le
Regard du roi*, completed *Dramouss* (translated as *A
Dream of Africa*). *Le Maître de la parole* (*The Guardian
of the Word*) appeared in 1978. Full of plans for future
projects, Camara Laye succumbed to illness and, in
1980, died at the age of fifty-two.

Camara Laye described *L'Enfant noir*—the story of
his rural childhood, his education in Guinea's capital
and later in Paris—as "what I am." *Dramouss* continues
the "what I am" project, keeping close to the author's
own life. In this novel a narrator returns to Guinea,
where he finds "a regime of anarchy and dictatorship, a
regime of violence"—words understood to have pro-
voked Sékou Touré. Camara Laye was never to write as
overtly politically again, but *Le Maître de la parole*
charts the life of the first emperor of the Kingdom of
Mali as told by griots, and can be read as a comment on
contemporary African politics.

The autobiographical groove Camara Laye settled into was violently disrupted just once. *Le Regard du roi* is his only fiction. To grasp the force of his talent as a novelist and to fully appreciate the singularity of his project, it is important to be alert to the cultural snares that entangle critical discourse about Africa. Shreds of the prejudices that menace Clarence cling to much of the novel's appraisal. In its explications, the language of criticism favors "spontaneous wisdom"[1] rather than strategy, spirit as distinct from the visible, comprehensible world; "mute symbols and cryptic messages"[2] over modern complexity; a naturalistic, universal humanism valued as a "gift to white readers"[3] over craftsmanship. Less attention is given to the book's pregnant dialogue; its delicate, almost clandestine, pacing; its carefully governed structure; to how the author's imagery deflates, alters, and addresses certain foundational European values; to his brilliant exploration of the concept of individual rights, the preeminence of money, and the bewildering obsession with the naked body.

Of the many literary tropes of Africa, three are invidious: Africa as jungle—impenetrable, chaotic, and threatening; Africa as sensual but not on its own rational; and the essence or "heart" of Africa, its ultimate

---

1. Albert S. Gérard, in his Introduction to *The Radiance of the King* (Macmillan, 1971), p. 19.

2. Sonia Lee, *Camara Laye* (Twayne, 1984), p. iii.

3. Gérard, Introduction, p. 20.

discovery, as, unless mitigated by European influence and education, incomprehensible. *The Radiance of the King* engages these concretized assessments in such a way that the reader is invited (not told) to reevaluate his or her own store of "knowledge."

It is fascinating to observe Camara Laye's adroit handling of certain elements of this mindscape. *Impenetrable Africa.* Clarence is afraid of the forest, seeing it as a wall, very much like the palace wall that appears to have no entrances, and as unnavigable as the maze of rooms through which he must make his escape. Because his trust in his companions is justifiably limited, he enters with trepidation. What he does not trust at all is his own sight. Although his companions exhibit no confusion, Clarence's fear is stupefying. In spite of noting that the forests are "devoted to wine industry," that the landscape is "cultivated," that the people living there give him a "cordial welcome," Clarence sees only inaccessibility, "common hostility," a vertigo of tunnels, invisible paths barred by thorn hedges. The order and clarity of the landscape are at odds with the menacing jungle in Clarence's head. "Where are the paths?" he cries. "There *are* paths," the beggar answers. "If you can't see them . . . you've only got your own eyes to blame."

Sensual Africa. Clarence's descent into acquiescent stud is a wry comment on the sensual basking that Europeans found so threatening. He enacts the full horror of what Westerners imagine as "going native," the "unclean and cloying weakness" that imperils masculinity. But Clarence's overt enjoyment of and feminine submission to continuous cohabitation reflect less the "dangers" of sexy Africa than the exposure of his willful blindness to a practical (albeit loathsome) enterprise. The night visits of the harem women (whom Clarence continues to believe against all evidence are one woman) are arranged by an impotent old man for the increase of his family rather than for Clarence's indulgence. The deceit is an achievement made possible by the Africans' quick understanding of this Frenchman's intellectual indolence, his tendency toward self-delusion. As mulatto children crowd the harem, Clarence, the only white in the region, continues to wonder where they came from.

Dark Africa. Although the novel is a revision of the white man's voyage into darkness, I do not see the journey, as some readers do, as a progression from European adult corruption to African childlike purity. Nor do the trials seem to imitate an Everyman's pilgrimage through sin and self-loathing necessary in order to effect an ultimate baptism. It appears to me that Clarence's voyage is *from* the metaphorical darkness of immaturity and degradation. Both of these crippling states precede his entrance into the narrative and are clearly dramatized by the adolescent stupidity with which he handles his affairs and the humiliation he has already suffered at the hands of his European compatriots. Camara Laye's

Africa is suffused with light: the watery green light of the forest; the blood-red tints of the houses and soil; the sky's "unbearable ... azure brilliance"; even the scales of the fish-women glimmer "like robes of dying moonlight."

The king's youth and Clarence's nakedness may encourage the reading of this novel as culminating with an inner child craving and receiving unearned yet limitless love. But the nakedness Clarence insists upon at the end is neither childish nor erotic. Nor is it "shamelessly immodest." It is stark, absolute—like a truth. " 'Because of your very nakedness!' the [king's] look seemed to say." He is accepted, loved, and called into view by the royal gaze because he has arrived at the juncture where truth, knowledge, is possible; where the "terrifying void that is within [him] ... opens to receive [the king]."

This openness, the crumbling of cultural armor and the evaporation of ego, is the beginning of an adult knowledge which is, of course, his salvation and his bliss. But deep in the heart of Africa's Africa is more than the restorative gaze of the king. There at its core is also equipoise—the radiance of his exquisite articulation: "Did you not know that I was waiting for you?"

Colm Tóibín on

THE GO-BETWEEN

BY L. P. HARTLEY

L. P. HARTLEY put everything he knew, and everything he was, into *The Go-Between*, which he published in 1953 when he was fifty-eight. He managed to dramatize his own watchful and uneasy presence in the world, his abiding concern with class and caste, and his very personal mixture of alarm and fascination at the body and the body's sexual needs and urges. It allowed him to evoke a past, a time half a century earlier, a golden age, as he saw it, of Victorian morals and manners, an age of innocence in the short time before its shattering. In *The Go-Between* he found the perfect way of making sense of his own complex relationship to class and sexuality and memory, but the novel's intensity also suggests that, working in a time when he alone seemed to possess rigid feelings about these matters, he was writing to save his life.

Leslie Poles Hartley was born in 1895 at a period when his father, who was a solicitor, was beginning to make his fortune from the brick industry. His parents were Methodists and Liberals, believing in self-improvement and good health and hard work. Hartley's

71

early years coincided with his family's move from the middle classes to the new rich, a move best symbolized by their purchase in 1900 of a miniature castle, Fletton, on the outskirts of Peterborough, in Cambridgeshire, a building that was to haunt and repel him for all of his life. In a letter to Lord David Cecil in 1971, a year before his death, he wrote: "Fletton, for some reason, is inimical to me. Whether my father was more severe than other Victorian parents I don't know—he certainly didn't mean to be—but I always felt at Fletton that I had done something wrong—especially in the North wing."

At his public school, Harrow, Hartley was the only boy from a family with Liberal political sympathies in his house, and his background in Wesleyan Methodism would have made his origins very clear to both his teachers and fellow students. Thus in his early teens he was handed a great gift for a novelist, something that may have made him personally unhappy but that allowed him to study the world as an outsider with a need to watch and learn and never feel comfortable. Hartley did not, however, enjoy his outsider status. By 1911 he was going for confirmation classes, and he subsequently became a member of the established church, the religion of his fellow Harrovians, the Church of England. All his life he felt this need to join the tribe, the upper class in England, with its extraordinary rules and snobberies. He put so much energy into moving himself, his whole being, from one class to another that it seemed to leave him exhausted. Thus when the English class system came under attack in the years after the First World War, Hartley was left defenseless. He never ceased to long for a Platonic England that he was sure had existed in his childhood and early youth, and his novels and stories play out the drama between his own uncertain status and his love and longing for a time of certainty, a world waiting to be broken, uncertainty made flesh.

Although he began to publish stories in his late twenties, he was mainly known as a book reviewer until the publication of his first novel, *The Shrimp and the Anemone*, in 1944, when he was almost fifty. He wrote for *The Nation, Saturday Review, The Weekend Review, The Observer*, and many other periodicals, and J.B. Priestley described him as "the best reviewer of fiction in the country." Hartley often read as many as five novels a week and reckoned that in all he must have read well over six thousand books.

Over these years he made two great discoveries. He found that he loved the company of louche aristocrats and made friends with many of them. And he discovered Venice, where he spent a great deal of time between 1922 and the beginning of the Second World War. He owned a gondola and employed a gondolier; he enjoyed, as much as any outsider could, Venetian society. *Simonetta Perkins*, his first substantial piece of fiction, published in 1925, deals with a young American woman who, having turned down offers of marriage, arrives in Venice with her sickly mother. (Hartley's own mother was a great hypochondriac.) She develops an enormous interest in a handsome gondolier called Emilio and tries to engage him for her sole use. Fellow Americans tell her that when the gondoliers have "relations" with certain tourists, "you may be sure they don't do it for nothing." Nonetheless, she decides to have relations with Emilio, and as she moves in this direction, courtesy of the gondola, one of Hartley's central preoccupations comes to be dramatized. His heroine's fascination with the possibilities of sex is mixed with fear, her longing darkened by a loathing for the very idea of coupling, a loathing that is all the more disabling for its being irrational and total. As she approaches the possibility of romantic fulfillment, "A wall of darkness, thought-proof and rigid like a fire-curtain, rattled down upon her consciousness. She was cut off from herself; a kind of fizzing, a ghastly mental effervescence, started in her head."

Hartley's early heroine has other echoes of the boy Leo in *The Go-Between*. She stands alone, quite unlike those around her, self-conscious and watchful, a subject of mockery. Hartley himself had reason to be acutely aware of his own effect on those around him. When Virginia Woolf was at Garsington, the home of Lady Ottoline Morrell, in the summer of 1923 in the company of Lord David Cecil, Puffin Asquith, and Eddy Sackville-West, she noted in her diary the presence of "a dull fat man called Hartley." Thirty years later, the writer and publisher John Calmann watched him sitting "like a delightful old pussy listening and purring contentedly. A pleasant man but so obsequious that I could not believe he really wrote [*The Go-Between*]." Sacheverell Sitwell's wife simply called him "Bore Hartley." He was not, it seems, the most exciting or comfortable companion. In photographs, he appears uneasy and withdrawn.

Nonetheless, he was a great host and weekend visitor, and his work suffered as he traveled and socialized. Hartley did not know how to shut himself away, and he managed to see a great deal of people whom he did not much like or who did not much like him. In one year he entertained forty-eight groups of houseguests. His homosexuality was known to most of those close to him, but he did not have a lover or companion. His mother, who lived until 1948, longed for his company and never ceased to want him to return to live in the family home. As time went by, Hartley drank more and began to dislike the filthy modern tide. He deplored jazz and motorcycles and swans (which impeded his boating activities) and the working class. He fought a great deal with his servants (and indeed with his publishers) and wrote many stories about relationships between masters and servants.

Leo, the narrator of *The Go-Between*, arrives at Brand-ham Hall in the hot summer of 1900 to stay with his school friend Marcus. A cautious boy being brought up frugally by his widowed mother, he enters the brave new world of the English aristocracy as Marian, the daughter of the big house, is having a love affair with Ted Burgess, a farmer at the other end of the class system. Leo, the outsider, becomes the bearer of messages between the two lovers.

The Go-Between has obvious autobiographical origins. In August 1909, for example, Hartley, who was staying with his school friend Moxey at Bradenham Hall in Norfolk, wrote to his mother, "I sleep with Moxey... and also with a dog, which at first reposed on the bed... On Saturday we had a ball, very grand indeed, at least, not very. We always have late dinner here. There is going to be a cricket-match today, the Hall against the village. I am going to score." A year later, he wrote to his mother from Hastings, where he was visiting a Mrs. Wallis, who wanted him to stay an extra day "as she wants me to go to a party... You know I am not very fond of parties and I do want to come home on Tuesday. However, they have asked me to write to you and ask if you would mind my staying. I am enjoying myself here but I am sure we should both prefer me to be at home. Of course if you think it would be better for me to stay, write to me and say so; it is only for a day. But still, I do want to be at home again." It is also clear from letters that the young Hartley, like Leo in *The Go-Between*, was not a good swimmer, though he was, like Leo, a good singer. Also, Hartley had worked as an army postman in the Great War and knew the thrill of delivering sought-after messages.

A novel is a thousand details, and any novelist will raid the past for moments that have resonance or ring true or may be useful, or simply come to mind easily and quickly. In his book *The Novelist's Responsibility* (1967), Hartley mused on the relationship between fiction and autobiography. He wrote that the novelist's world "must, in some degree, be an extension of his own life; its fundamental problems must be his problems, its preoccupations his preoccupations—or something allied to them." He also warned that while it is "unsafe to assume that a novelist's work is autobiographical in any direct sense," it is nonetheless "plausible to assume that his work is a transcription, an anagram of his own experience, reflecting its shape and tone and tempo."

His experience when he began *The Go-Between* in Venice in May 1952 was that of a man who remained uncomfortable in his chosen milieu, who had learned a set of rules to help him belong. Nothing was taken for granted. He had studiously avoided intimacy. Thus he would have no difficulty describing a middle-class boy's visit to a grand house, a boy with a brittle consciousness who was wearing unsuitable clothes, open to ridicule, watching everything so he could learn and not be laughed at, a boy who would be mortally wounded by a display of intimacy. Hartley was ready to explore what he described in *The Novelist's Responsibility* as "this idea or situation" that goes on in a writer "like a kind of murmur; it is what their thoughts turn to when they are by themselves."

Hartley worked on *The Go-Between* with an intensity unique in his writing life, remaining alone in a Venice that seemed to him increasingly alien, leaving behind an England that seemed like a foreign country. In June, he wrote to a friend: "I began to write a novel: this has occupied me rather obsessively—indeed, there *was* a moment when, if I had kept the pace up, I should almost have rivaled Stendhal who . . . wrote the Chartreuse de Parme in about six months . . . Now I have slowed down, but still done quite a big chunk." By October, the book was finished and he began to revise it.

Later, he wrote that he "didn't choose the year 1900 for its period possibilities. I wanted to evoke the feeling of that summer, the long stretch of fine weather, and also the confidence in life, the belief that all's well with the world, which everyone enjoyed or seemed to enjoy before the First World War . . . The Boer War was a local affair, and so I was able to set my little private tragedy against a general background of security and happiness." It was vital for Hartley to believe, as his world crumbled, that he had known such an England and could evoke it quickly, simply, effortlessly. Thus the relationship of weather to landscape, of servant to master, of village to big house, of England to Empire is perfectly in place. Only two things are not, and these become the novel's subject: Leo is out of place, and Hartley can describe that feeling in sensuous detail, moment by Proustian moment, down to the meals, the voices, the newcomers, the quality of the heat, and the quality of his own discomfort. The book's power arises from the boy's rich way of noticing, his desperate attempt to become a reliable narrator, absorbing and recounting detail and episode and sweet sensation. He is especially alert to the prospect of humiliation, on the lookout for mockery or attack.

Out of place too is the secret love affair between Marian and Ted. It is clear from letters and articles that Hartley disapproved of their affair and expected the reader to do so as well. He set out, he wrote, to produce "a story of innocence betrayed, and not only betrayed but corrupted." When he gave a talk at Leicester a few months after the book's publication, he was surprised to discover that his audience had sympathy with Marian and Ted. "I wonder," he wrote to his publisher, "what the Midlands are coming to."

The Midlands, however, had drawn their inspiration directly from Hartley himself, who had softened the character of Marian and indeed that of Ted as he worked on the book and had been too interested in the aura of uncontrolled sensuality between them to bother disapproving of them. It is fascinating to watch a novelist working against the grain of his or her own belief, finding a set of compulsions in the imagination or in the most secret and hidden parts of the self that will obliterate mere opinion.

The writing is full of sensuous detail. "And the heat was a medium which made this change of outlook possible. As a liberating power with its own laws it was outside my experience. In the heat the commonest objects changed their nature. Walls, trees, the very ground one trod on, instead of being cool were warm to the touch: and the sense of touch is the most transfiguring of all the senses." Leo, like the American in Venice twenty-five years earlier in *Simonetta Perkins*, longs for liberation and transfiguration. He carries his longing with him as he carries Marian and Ted's letters: "I carried about with me something that made me dangerous, but what it was and why it made me dangerous, I had no idea." The pull within Hartley himself between his hidden sensuous nature and his love of cold dry order is played out in the cricket match that Leo sees as "the struggle between order and lawlessness, between obedience to tradition and defiance of it, between social stability and revolution, between one attitude to life and another. I knew which side I was on; yet the traitor within my gates felt the issue differently, he backed the individual against the side, even my own side . . ."

Hartley's imagination softening his own strictures was the traitor within the gates. In an essay on Henry

James, he remarked that James "would never have written a novel which seemed to mitigate the sin of adultery." Hartley sought to put everything he knew, or thought he knew, about boyhood and England and class into *The Go-Between*, and add, for good measure, the sin of adultery and its corrupting effect. Slowly, however, as he worked, he seemed to argue with himself, so that the reader is left with the love between Marian and Ted as a great fierce love, worthy of a writer who admired Emily Brontë as much as Hartley did.

He understood, like Leo, the sense of treachery that can be felt by an outsider in a group, but he also began to work with something more mysterious and powerful—a treachery within the self, a treachery conjured into existence by the power of the flesh, by a seductive strength that cannot be resisted, and that stands at the root of life itself. This was a subject that would preoccupy many English novelists of Hartley's generation, including D. H. Lawrence and E. M. Forster, the idea that the senses, in all their heat and spontaneity, were the only useful weapons to withstand the demands of strict, dull, deathly English duty. Hartley the citizen was on the side of England; Hartley working on *The Go-Between* was not so sure.

Thus in Chapter 15 when Leo finds Ted in his kitchen "with a gun between his knees, so absorbed that he didn't hear me," it is clear that he is in the presence of a powerful and irresistible force. Just as he had been transformed by Marian's attention, now he is ready to bask in Ted's raw sexual power. The reader cannot resist wanting Ted and Marian to prevail because Leo cannot resist either of them. He is longing for them with all the more zeal and passion because he will be destroyed and pulled under by them and will not recover. He watches Ted, "the muscles of his forearms ... moved in ridges and hollows from a knot above the elbow, like pistons working from a cylinder" as "he pushed the wire rod up and down" while cleaning his gun. Ted makes him hold the gun. "I got a strange thrill from the contact, from feeling the butt press against my shoulder and the steel cold against my palm."

The meeting between them is sodden with sexual charge. Hartley erased a later passage in which Ted teaches Leo to swim: "I could hardly wait to get my clothes off. The impulse towards nudity which had assailed me ever since I came to Trimingham, the longing, half physical, half spiritual, to get everything off, to feel the sun on my skin, to have nothing between me and the elements, to be at one with the summer, now had the compulsion of a passion ... The galloping approach of fulfilment drummed in my ears; I tingled with expectancy." With Ted as his teacher, Leo comes to feel the freedom of the water, "a freedom which the touch of his hand, guiding me this way and that, keeping the soft pull of gravity at bay, did nothing to diminish."

Hartley was right to cut this passage. It made too

much too clear. It is, in any case, written between the lines of the book, which turns out not to be a drama about class or about England, or a lost world mourned by Hartley; instead it is a drama about Leo's deeply sensuous nature moving blindly, in a world of rich detail and beautiful sentences, toward a destruction that is impelled by his own intensity of feeling and, despite everything, his own innocence.

Francine Prose on

A HIGH WIND IN JAMAICA

BY RICHARD HUGHES

FIRST THE vague premonitory chill—familiar, seductive, unwelcome—then the syrupy aura coating the visible world, through which its colors and edges appear
ever more lurid and sharp... The experience of reading Richard Hughes's *A High Wind in Jamaica* (a book
in which swoons and febrile states play a critical role)
evokes the somatic sensations of falling ill, as a child.
Indeed it recalls much about childhood that we thought
(or might have wished) we had forgotten, while it labors
with sly intelligence to dismantle the moral constructs
that our adult selves have so painstakingly assembled.

The book opens among the ruined houses of the
West Indies, slave quarters and mansions democratically
leveled by "earthquake, fire, rain, and deadlier vegeta-
tion," and features a frightening cameo appearance of
the Misses Parkers, a pair of bedridden elderly heiresses
starved to death by their servants amid ormolu clocks
and the bloodied feathers of slaughtered chickens. The
scene is grim, fantastical, but the novel's language is
delicate and precise—there is a humorous, chirpy cer-
ebration to its narrative voice—and right away we are

conscious of, and troubled by, the dissonance between tone and content—one that turns out, however, to be central to the shocking story Hughes has to tell. For on the surface, *A High Wind in Jamaica* is an adventure yarn involving five British children captured by a crew of pirates. But underneath this high-spirited romp is a story about murder, senseless violence, gothic sexuality, and capricious betrayal, a narrative that more nearly evokes the pictures of the "outsider" artist Henry Darger than those of, say, Kate Greenaway.

When we first meet the Bas-Thornton family, they are living in Jamaica, where Mr. Thornton is involved in "business of some kind." The children have business of their own, most of it involving the serial cruelty with which they treat the island's hapless indigenous fauna. In this "paradise for English children," John, the eldest son, catches rats for the degustation and sport of Tabby, the family's half-wild pet cat, itself fond of mortal combat with poisonous snakes. Emily, the oldest of three girls, whose deeply peculiar experience and consciousness is at the center of the novel, has a passion for "catching house-lizards without their dropping their tails off, which they do when frightened. . . . Her room was full of these and other pets, some alive, others probably dead."

The younger Thorntons' sphere is so distant—so different—from that of their parents that they might as well be feral children. Mr. and Mrs. Thornton have no idea who their offspring are, or about the steamy, highly charged dramas that they are secretly enacting. "This sort of life was very peaceful, and might be excellent for nervy children like John; but a child like Emily, thought Mrs. Thornton, who is far from nervy, really needs some sort of stimulus and excitement, or there is a danger of her mind going to sleep altogether for ever. This life was too vegetable." It takes a typhoon blowing the roof off the family house—an event upstaged for the children by Tabby's murder by a pack of wild cats amidst thunder and lightning—before the grown-up Thorntons decide that the island life really is unsuitable, and send their brood off to Britain on the *Clorinda*.

By this point, Hughes has subjected us to a kind of Pavlovian conditioning: every time an animal appears, we brace ourselves for the worst. But even this protective recoil cannot quite prepare us for the grisly scene in which the crew of the *Clorinda* attempts to amputate a monkey's cancerous tail—and in the ensuing mayhem, are overtaken and captured by pirates. Nor can we possibly anticipate the brutality that transpires later, while the pirates are pleasantly occupied with their riotous efforts to make the circus lion and tiger fight. Throughout the book, both nature and human nature are sinister, threatening. The physicality of animal life—when Emily goes for a swim, "hundreds of infant fish were tickling with their inquisitive mouths every inch of her body, a sort of expressionless light kissing"—is "abominable." The setting sun—"unusually large and red, as if he threatened something peculiar"—seems predatory and perverted. The children themselves are, essentially, animate Petri dishes in which a "diabolic yeast" proliferates, and our initial fondness for the bumbling pirates is tempered by some nasty scenes. Captain Jonsen's drunken display of murky attention leads Emily to defend herself by biting his thumb, and later there is a creepy moment when he looks in on the sleeping children and, knowing that Emily is awake and watching, flicks his fingernail against baby Laura's bare and upraised bottom.

Hughes is not afraid to dwell on startling, uncomfortable verities about the world and its inhabitants, and one of the things he does most impressively in *A High Wind in Jamaica* is to put a wicked spin on the Romantic notion of the child—the Wordsworthian innocent-savant. He suggests that children are closer than adults to nature, that the way that they view sex—mysterious, fascinating, incomprehensible, repulsive, responsible for weird alliances and even stranger behavior—is the way sex really is. Passion between consenting adults is a polite convention compared to the immediate realities of the flashy, "twittering" drag queens who assist the pirates in the capture of the *Clorinda*, or the night Emily gets to spend in bed with a pet alligator, or the suffocating kisses little Edward receives from a fat, mustachioed old woman who grabs him during the pirates' Cuban layover. ("Edward could no more have struggled than if caught by a boa. Moreover, the portentous woman fascinated him, as if she had been a boa indeed. He lay in her arms limp, self-conscious, and dejected: but without active thought of escape.")

The confusions and seductions, horrors and comforts of Emily's relationship with the captain, and later with the bewitching Louisa Dawson—a passenger on the steamer to which the pirates eventually surrender the children, and which brings them to England—belong to the same polymorphous realm of attraction and repugnance as her encounter with the kissing fish. The captain amuses himself by drawing the sort of sexual doodles that might be done by a young boy. At one point he draws over the figures Emily has penciled on the wall of her bunk:

> Jonsen could only draw two things: ships, and naked women. . . . He took the pencil: and before long there began to appear between Emily's crude uncertain lines round thighs, rounder bellies, high swelling bosoms, all somewhat in the manner of Rubens.

This scene of a grown man amending a girl's scribblings has an upsetting, sensational edge that recalls a child's skewed perspective on physicality; it is all the more disturbing for its weird aspect of innocence.

If adult sexuality seems unhealthily like a child's, adult morality is hardly more mature or developed. Everyone lies and keeps poisonous secrets, especially the children. ("Grown-ups embark on a life of deception with considerable misgivings, and generally fail. But not so children. A child can hide the most appalling secret without the least effort, and is practically secure against detection.") Everyone, of every age, behaves according to an almost psychotically private and individual set of moral criteria: it's wrong to mention underwear and call adults by their first names but permissible (or hardly worth noting) to lie to God in one's prayers and misdirect a court of law convened to try a capital offense. No one has much of a memory; the children adapt quickly to separation from their parents and recover from the shock of a death among them with alarming ease and flexibility.

By the end of the book, what the children have been told about their ordeal by the adults (who themselves have little or no interest in the truth) has blended with, or replaced, their sense of what really occurred. And when we meet the lawyers directing the trial that occupies the final section of the novel, we realize that these representatives of justice and high civilization—after all that wildness!—are little better than pirates in robes and periwigs. They are men, Hughes slyly informs us, whose interest in the world is the opposite of a writer's: "It is the novelist who is concerned with facts, whose job it is to say what a particular man did do on a particular occasion: the lawyer does not, cannot be expected to go further than to show what the ordinary man would be most likely to do under presumed circumstances."

Unlike William Golding's far more simplistic *The Lord of the Flies*, to which it is sometimes compared, Richard Hughes's novel resists any attempts to extract from it a moral or sociological lesson, a bit of received wisdom or home truth. It's hard, in fact, to think of another fiction so blithe in its refusal to throw us the tiniest crumb of solace or consolation, to present a single character who functions as a lodestar of rectitude or beneficence.

In the end, everything in this luminous, extraordinary novel is so much the reverse of what we think it should be, or what we would expect, that we are left entirely disoriented—unsure of what anything is, or should be. The effect is disturbing and yet beautiful, fantastic but also frighteningly true to life. Published in 1929, just as history was preparing events that would forever revise the terms in which one could talk about innocence and evil, *A High Wind in Jamaica* is one of those prescient works of art that seems somehow to have caught (on the breeze, as it were) a warning scent of danger and blood—that is to say, of the future.

Susan Sontag on

LETTERS: SUMMER 1926

BY BORIS PASTERNAK, MARINA TSVETAYEVA, AND RAINER MARIA RILKE

WHAT IS happening in 1926, when the three poets are writing to one another?

On May 12, Shostakovich's Symphony No. 1 in F Minor is heard for the first time, performed by the Leningrad Philharmony; the composer is nineteen years old.

On June 10, the elderly Catalan architect Antonio Gaudí, on the walk he takes every day from the construction site of the Cathedral of the Sagrada Familia to a church in the same neighborhood in Barcelona for vespers, is hit by a trolley, lies unattended on the street (because, it's said, nobody recognizes him), and dies.

On August 6, Gertrude Ederle, nineteen years old, American, swims from Cap Griz-Nez, France, to Kingsdown, England, in fourteen hours and thirty-one minutes, becoming the first woman to swim the English Channel and the first woman competing in a major sport to best the male record-holder.

On August 23, the movie idol Rudolph Valentino dies of endocarditis and septicemia in a hospital in New York.

SUSAN SONTAG

On September 3, a steel Broadcasting Tower (Funk-turm), 138 meters high with restaurant and panorama platform, is inaugurated in Berlin.

Some books: Volume Two of Hitler's *Mein Kampf*, Hart Crane's *White Buildings*, A. A. Milne's *Winnie the Pooh*, Viktor Shklovsky's *Third Factory*, Louis Aragon's *Le Paysan de Paris*, D. H. Lawrence's *The Plumed Serpent*, Hemingway's *The Sun Also Rises*, Agatha Christie's *The Murder of Roger Ackroyd*, T. E. Lawrence's *The Seven Pillars of Wisdom*.

A few films: Fritz Lang's *Metropolis*, Vsevolod Pudovkin's *Mother*, Jean Renoir's *Nana*, Herbert Brenon's *Beau Geste*.

Two plays: Bertolt Brecht's *Mann ist Mann* and Jean Cocteau's *Orphée*.

On December 6, Walter Benjamin arrives for a two-month stay in Moscow. He does not meet the thirty-six-year-old Boris Pasternak.

Pasternak has not seen Marina Tsvetayeva for four years. Since she left Russia in 1922, they have become each other's most cherished interlocutor and Pasternak, tacitly acknowledging Tsvetayeva as the greater poet, has made her his first reader.

Tsvetayeva, who is thirty-four, is living in penury with her husband and two children in Paris.

Rilke, who is fifty-one, is dying of leukemia in a sanatorium in Switzerland.

Letters: Summer 1926 is a portrait of the sacred delir-
ium of art. There are three participants: a god and
two worshipers, who are also worshipers of each other
(and who we, the readers of their letters, know to be future gods).

A pair of young Russian poets, who have exchanged
years of fervent letters about work and life, enter into
correspondence with a great German poet who, for both,
is poetry incarnate. These three-way love letters—and
they are that—are an incomparable dramatization of
ardor about poetry and about the life of the spirit.

They portray a domain of reckless feeling and purity
of aspiration which it would be our loss to dismiss as
"romantic."

The literatures written in German and in Russian
have been particularly devoted to spiritual exaltation.
Tsvetayeva and Pasternak know German, and Rilke has
studied and attained a passable mastery of Russian—all
three suffused by the dreams of literary divinity promul-
gated in these languages. The Russians, lovers of German poetry and music since childhood (the mothers of
both were pianists), expect the greatest poet of the age
to be someone writing in the language of Goethe and
Hölderlin. And the German-language poet has had as a
formative early love and mentor a writer, born in St.
Petersburg, with whom he traveled twice to Russia, ever

since which he has considered that country his true, spiritual homeland.

On the second of these trips, in 1900, Pasternak actually saw and probably was presented to the young Rilke.

Pasternak's father, the celebrated painter, was an esteemed acquaintance; Boris, the future poet, was ten years old. It is with the sacred memory of Rilke boarding a train with his lover Lou Andreas-Salomé—they remain, reverently, unnamed—that Pasternak begins *Safe Conduct* (1931), his supreme achievement in prose.

Tsvetayeva, of course, has never set eyes on Rilke.

All three poets are agitated by seemingly incompatible needs: for the most absolute solitude and for the most intense communion with another like-minded spirit. "My voice can ring out pure and clear only when absolutely solitary," Pasternak tells his father in a letter. Ardor inflected by intransigence drives all of Tsvetayeva's writings. In "Art in the Light of Conscience" (1932), she writes:

> The poet can have only one prayer: not to understand the unacceptable—let me not understand, so that I may not be seduced . . . let me not hear, so that I may not answer . . . The poet's only prayer is a prayer for deafness.

And the signature two-step of Rilke's life, as we know from his letters to a variety of correspondents, mostly women, is flight from intimacy and a bid for unconditional sympathy and understanding.

Although the younger poets announce themselves as acolytes, the letters quickly become an exchange of equals, a competition of affinities. To those familiar with the main branches of Rilke's grandiose, often stately correspondence it may come as a surprise to find him responding in almost the same eager, jubilant tones as his two Russian admirers. But never has he had interlocutors of this caliber. The sovereign, didactic Rilke we know from the *Letters to a Young Poet*, written between 1903 and 1908, has disappeared. Here is only angelic conversation. Nothing to teach. Nothing to learn.

Opera is the only medium now in which it is still acceptable to rhapsodize. The duo that concludes Richard Strauss's *Ariadne auf Naxos*, whose libretto is by one of Rilke's contemporaries, Hugo von Hofmannsthal, offers a comparable effusiveness. We are surely more comfortable with the paean to love as rebirth and self-transformation sung by Ariadne and Bacchus than with the upsurges of amorous feeling declared by the three poets.

And these letters are not concluding duos. They are duos trying, and eventually failing, to be trios. What kind of possession of each other do the poets expect? How consuming and how exclusive is this kind of love?

The correspondence has begun, with Pasternak's father as the intermediary, between Rilke and Pasternak.

SUSAN SONTAG

Then Pasternak suggests to Rilke that he write to
Tsvetayeva, and the situation becomes a correspondence
à trois. Last to enter the lists, Tsvetayeva quickly becomes the igniting force, so powerful, so outrageous
are her need, her boldness, her emotional nakedness.
Tsvetayeva is the relentless one, outgalloping first Pasternak, then Rilke. Pasternak, who no longer knows
what to demand of Rilke, retreats (and Tsvetayeva also
calls a halt to *their* correspondence); Tsvetayeva can
envisage an erotic, engulfing tie. Imploring Rilke to con-
sent to a meeting, she succeeds only in driving him
away. Rilke, in his turn, falls silent. (His last letter to
her is on August 19.)

The flow of rhetoric reaches the precipice of the sub-
lime, and topples over into hysteria, anguish, dread.

But, curiously, death seems quite unreal. How aston-
ished and shattered the Russians are when this "phe-
nomenon of nature" (so they thought of Rilke) is in
some sense no more. Silence should be full. Silence
which now has the name of death seems too great a
diminishment.

So the correspondence has to continue.

Tsvetayeva writes a letter to Rilke a few days after
being told he has died at the end of December, and
addresses a long prose ode to him ("Your Death") the
following year. The manuscript of *Safe Conduct*, which
Pasternak completes almost five years after Rilke's
death, ends with a letter to Rilke. ("If you were alive,

this is the letter I would send you today.") Leading the reader through a labyrinth of elliptical memoiristic prose to the core of the poet's inwardness, *Safe Conduct* is written under the sign of Rilke and, if only unconsciously, in competition with Rilke, being an attempt to match if not surpass *The Notebooks of Malte Laurids Brigge* (1910), Rilke's supreme achievement in prose.

Early in *Safe Conduct*, Pasternak speaks of living on and for those occasions when "a complete feeling burst into space with the whole extent of space before it." Never has a brief for the powers of lyric poetry been made so brilliantly, so rapturously, as in these letters. Poetry cannot be abandoned or renounced, once you are "the lyre's thrall," Tsvetayeva instructs Pasternak in a letter of July 1925. "With poetry, dear friend, as with love; no separation until it drops you."

Or until death intervenes. Tsvetayeva and Pasternak haven't suspected that Rilke was seriously ill. Learning that he has died, the two poets are incredulous: it seems, cosmically speaking, unjust. And fifteen years later Pasternak would be surprised and remorseful when he received the news of Tsvetayeva's suicide in August 1941. He hadn't, he admitted, grasped the inevitability of the doom that awaited her if she decided to return to the Soviet Union with her family, as she did in 1939.

Separation had made everything replete. What would Rilke and Tsvetayeva have said to each other had they actually met? We know what Pasternak *didn't* say to

Tsvetayeva when they were briefly reunited after thirteen years, in June 1935, on the day he arrived in Paris in the nightmarish role of official Soviet delegate to the International Writers Congress for the Defense of Culture: he didn't warn her not to come back, not to think of coming back, to Moscow.

Maybe the ecstasies channeled into this correspondence could only have been voiced in separateness, and in response to the ways in which they failed one another. (As the greatest writers invariably demand too much of, and are failed by, readers.) Nothing can dim the incandescence of those exchanges over a few months in 1926 when they were hurling themselves at one another, making their impossible, glorious demands. Today, when "all is drowning in Pharisaism"—the phrase is Pasternak's—their ardors and their tenacities feel like raft, beacon, beach.

Luc Sante on

CLASSIC CRIMES

BY WILLIAM ROUGHEAD

THE GENRE we call "true crime," obviously one of the very oldest in literature, has, despite a biblical pedigree, spent much of its career in the literary slums. The genre from which it is adjectivally distinguished —although seldom referred to as "false crime"—has produced classics as well as potboilers, but the nonfictional narrative of crime has chiefly been associated with such raffish vehicles as the ballad broadside, the penny-dreadful, the tabloid extra, the pulp detective magazine, and the current pestilence of paperbacks uniform in their one-sentence paragraphs, two-word titles, and covers with black backgrounds, white letters, and obligatory splash of blood. There's really nothing wrong with any of these—even the current paperbacks are bound to seem more charming as time passes. Still, you might wonder: Where is the Homer of true crime, its Cervantes, its Dostoevsky?

William Roughead might at least be its Henry James. The two were friends and correspondents, and they shared a variety of interests and inclinations: complex characters, hopelessly tangled motives, labyrinths of nuance, arcane language, byzantine sentence structure. Roughead was a Scotsman who was born in 1870 and died in 1952, although the unknowing reader would be forgiven for ascribing to him a set of dates several decades earlier, so resolutely unmodern is his prose—not that it is in any way stiff, cold, musty, or particularly quaint. He began his career at twenty-three as a Writer to the Signet, a term that has no literary implication, referring rather to an elite body of Scottish attorneys. His passion for the law extended well beyond his actual duties. As he notes in passing several times herein, he was from his youth both a frequent spectator at major trials and an indefatigable collector of newspaper clippings on criminal cases that interested him, and he went on to edit a number of the volumes in the celebrated Notable British Trials series, then to collect his commentaries in books issued by a small press in Edinburgh. His works were taken up by a commercial publisher only when he was in his sixties.

So mercantile calculation clearly played no part in determining his choice of pursuits. His was one of those astoundingly ambitious Edwardian hobbies that differed from professions only in their lack of financial compensation—it was a time when every retired general seemed to be translating Hesiod and every diplomat apparently had a sideline in paleontology. In Roughead we can observe the most sophisticated and refined expression of the British middle-class armchair fascination with crime. When, in "The West Port Murders," Roughead invites us to look over his shoulder at "an inch-square bit of brown leather" that is in fact a fragment of the tanned skin of the murderer and ghoul William Burke, handed down by the author's grandfather, the scene—we imagine Roughead wearing a dressing gown and a velvet cap, examining the grisly relic with a bone-handled magnifying glass—contains in full that collision, of placid, well-furnished, and obsessively well-organized pedantry with savage howling atavism, that is the keynote of that fascination.

Virtually all the hallmarks of the classic British mystery appear here, the apparent originals of those overly clever poisonings, those horrors in sleepy priories and dramas set against majestic Highland backdrops, those appallingly unlikely suspects and convenient foreign scapegoats, those algebra-problem alibi timetables, those ever-present watchful servants, those pathetically mundane overlooked clues. These cases have an advantage over their fictional descendants, however, by virtue of their mess, complication, frequent lack of satisfactory closure, and of course their psychological depth. They are anything but cozy. Roughead is not especially interested in clever paradoxes and neat resolutions; in fact he is not nearly as fascinated by the clue-hunting and deductive cogitation aspects of his cases as he is by their elaboration in the courtroom. A murder for him is of interest chiefly insofar as it provides the premise for a rich, complex trial at which personalities can clash, unfold, reveal their wrinkles.

Personality is the tie that binds together these twelve otherwise relatively disparate cases, which are mostly murders but not all, and are mostly but not all set in Scotland. Roughead writes about cases he observed himself, but he also delves into the archived transcripts and writes vividly of cases that took place a century or more before his birth. The protagonist can be obviously guilty, or obviously guilty but nevertheless released or acquitted, or falsely accused, or even, as in "Katharine Nairn," not accused at all, as the slippery Anne Clark steals every scene of that particular show, despite its title. At their best, trial transcripts combine theatrical movement, interplay, and suspense with the voyeuristic fascination presented by someone else's open trunk. They can supply all the ingredients for a sophisticated and modernistically jagged portrait, but it takes someone like Roughead to know how to extract and display those ingredients without losing momentum to procedural detours and longueurs—courtroom scenes have, after all, produced some of the most deadly boring stretches in movie history.

Roughead, with his jeweler's eye for extravagantly serpentine characters, his taste for unresolvable conflicts, self-devouring schemes, and barely decipherable motives, his pleasure in stories that disdain such conventions as a clear-cut beginning, middle, and end, is

something of a cubist posing as a fogey. His own personality, vivid at every moment even when he is not
actually an actor in the scene, is fundamental to his
strategy, and to his charm. He is certainly no shrinking
violet, and neither is he one of those rigorously deadpan
journalists who insist on letting the facts speak for
themselves. He is at once stage manager, color commen-
tator, handicapper, gossip, and final-appeals judge. He is
relentlessly discursive, his asides convincingly sounding
as if they are being whispered along a bench, and digressive too. But his sense of timing is superb: though he'll
take the reader on a walk through the past or through
the neighborhood, he will always be back in time for the
crucial next question. There are, to be sure, thickets of
local reference and forgotten allusion, and he seldom
fails to introduce a barrister without summarizing the
now obscure highlights of his illustrious later career, but
the reader can simply file these under "atmosphere."

His prose represents the full range of the English language, circa 1880, as played on a cathedral organ with
the largest possible number of manuals, pedals, and
stops. He traffics in rare words, disused expressions,
abstruse variants, and strictly local idioms, deploying
them for reasons that are sometimes historical, sometimes psychological, often shamelessly musical. You
can open the book anywhere and light on a random sentence—for instance, "The secret marauder came and
went without a trace, save for the empty till, the rifled

scrutoire, or the displenished plate-chest that testified to his visitation." Numerous ways exist of expressing this thought that would convey all the essential information in fewer and more austere terms, but that "scrutoire," that "displenished" have a majesty about them that at once relates to the magnificence of the marauder's character—the flamboyant Deacon Brodie—and gives a glimpse of his times, the 1780s. And anyway, the sentence gives pleasure, well beyond any question of utility. The usages herein may often send the reader to the dictionary, sometimes even to the OED. The word does not even have to be unusual in itself; I was baffled by his use of "ghostly" (as in "Constance Kent . . . was admitted an inmate of St. Mary's Home . . . under the ghostly ward of the Rev. Arthur Wagner . . .") until I realized that Roughead invariably employs it as a synonym for "spiritual."

These are twelve strong stories. One of them, the tale of the ghouls Burke and Hare, will be familiar to most readers, at least in outline, from Robert Louis Stevenson's *The Body Snatcher* (and its superb 1945 Val Lewton film adaptation). The rest are discoveries: "Katharine Nairn" discloses the chaos and squalor of the eighteenth-century Scottish gentry. Madeleine Smith might be the template of the lethal film noir heroine. The belowstairs drama of "The Sandyford Mystery" all but calls for a floor plan and a stopwatch. "Dr. Pritchard" deserves a stage performance and "The Arran

Murder" suggests a great lost Hitchcock movie. If the Balham mystery is something of a black hole, the Ard-lamont and Merrett mysteries are black comedies, their defendants' respective tissues of lies so thin and apparently permeable that the wonder is how they thought they could fool anyone—but they did. And finally there is the bizarre, protracted miscarriage of justice that is the case of Oscar Slater, one that invites the usual misuse of the adjective "Kafkaesque." Here, as in a number of the cases, Roughead's barely controlled outrage in the face of injustice—to the point where he becomes an actor in his own story—reveals that he was no mere vicarious bloodshed buff but an idealist and even a crusader. Such a combination of gifts and attributes as Roughead possessed is seldom found in writers of any description, and it is probably safe to say that they have never otherwise been brought together in the practice of that unfairly déclassé genre, true crime.

James Wood on

THE GOLOVLYOV FAMILY

BY SHCHEDRIN

THE HYPOCRITE may serve, among other things, as a deformed ambassador of the truth. By so obviously misrepresenting the truth, he enables us to trace its smothered outlines. In fiction and drama, this traditional hypocrite acts rather like an unreliable narrator. The unreliable narrator is rarely truly unreliable, because his unreliability is manipulated by an author, without whose reliable manipulation we would not be able to take the narrator's measure. As the unreliable narrator is really only a reliably unreliable narrator, so the traditional hypocrite is always reliably hypocritical, which is why we are so unthreatened by—indeed so enjoy the prospect of—Polonius, Tartuffe, Parson Adams, Pecksniff, and others. Such characters are comic and certify our rectitude, giving us pleasure that, whatever we have become, we have not become that kind of person. Though in a curious, unintended way, if we are not careful, such characters may turn us into hypocrites: the content and well-fed audiences watching Molière suggest that this has already happened.

We can see through the traditional hypocrite because

his zeal tends to be a perversion, almost a parody, of a visible moral code. He is nourished by the same food we consume; but, as it were, he eats far too much of it, and has become bullyingly large. Yet what would the hypocrite represent in a world starved of moral nutrition? A world in which the moral code has already been perverted, long before the hypocrite gets to it? Such a character becomes much more menacing than the traditional hypocrite, for there is no longer any truth for him reliably to misrepresent, and our reading of his motives becomes more difficult. He becomes opaque to us precisely because he ceases to be "a hypocrite," and he ceases to be a hypocrite because he is not a liar: there is nothing for him to lie about. Accordingly, he would be more likely to be a tragic than a comic figure, and more likely to be a solipsist or fantasist than a liar. He has merged with his own horrid world; he has no audience.

In his extraordinary novel *The Golovlyov Family*, the Russian writer Shchedrin (the nom de plume of M. E. Saltykov, sometimes known as Saltykov-Shchedrin) depicts just such a character and just such a world. The hypocrite is Porphyry Golovlyov, one of the sons of Arina Petrovna and Vladimir Mikhaylovich Golovlyov, and the novel, called by D. S. Mirsky "certainly the gloomiest in all Russian literature," is set on the Golovlyovs' dismal estate, known as Golovlyovo. The Golovlyovs are minor landowners (a class Shchedrin satirized in many stories and sketches, and from which he himself came), who, supported by the labor of their serfs, squander a privilege of which they are unaware.

Vladimir, the father, spends most of his time in his study, drinking, imitating the songs of starlings, and writing bawdy verse, while the estate is run by his wife, the ferociously continent and cruel Arina Petrovna. She has little but contempt for her three sons, especially the eldest and youngest, Stepan and Pavel. But for her middle son, Porphyry, known from early days to his family as Little Judas or Bloodsucker, she also feels something like fear. Even when the child was a baby, "he liked to behave affectionately to his 'dear friend mamma,' to kiss her unobtrusively on the shoulder and sometimes to tell tales. . . . But even in those early days Arina Petrovna felt as it were suspicious of her son's ingratiating ways. Even at that time the gaze that he fixed at her seemed to her enigmatic, and she could not decide what precisely was in it —venom or filial respect."

Golovlyovo is a house of death. One by one the members of the family try to escape, and one by one they return and die. Of course, they only come home because they are in desperate straits. Thus, having run through a family allowance, Stepan arrives from Moscow, only forty but looking a decade older, "inflamed by drink and rough weather," his eyes bulging and bloodshot: "He looked about him morosely from under his brows; this was due not to any inward discontent, but rather to a vague fear that at any minute he might suddenly drop dead with hunger." Stepan hopes to squeeze a little more life out of the family estate, but the punitive Arina, who has her own survival to think of, rations her indulgence.

Stepan is already dying, in a sense. On the Golovlyov estate, where everyone is barely hanging on to existence, the best means of survival is a kind of shutting down of the moral system, as the body sleeps in very cold weather. Thus, the commonest emotion at Golovlyovo is the moral equivalent of boredom: an empty blindness. Stepan, for instance, is described thus: "He had not a single thought, not a single desire. . . . He wanted nothing, nothing at all." His mother is no less sealed off. She allows Stepan a diet that is just sufficient to keep him from starving, and when she is told that he is ailing, the words do "not reach her ears or make any impression upon her mind." For Arina has the Golovlyov disease: "She had lost all sight of the fact that next door to her, in the office, lived a man related to her by blood."

Likewise, Pavel, who locks himself away and drinks himself to death, is described as "an apathetic, mutely sullen man whose character was purely negative and never expressed itself in action," and as "the most perfect instance of a man devoid of any characteristics at all." And near the end of the book, when Porphyry's niece, Anninka, also returns to die, she spends the time pacing up and down, "singing in an undertone and trying to tire herself out and, above all, not to think."

Golovlyovo is a place of evil in the sense that Augustine and Calvin understood evil: as nothingness, the absence of goodness. The religious emphasis is proper, for in this vacated world, the man who briefly prospers, Little Judas, is above all a brilliant manipulator of religious hypocrisy. He fills the abyss with a diabolic version of traditional religion. Once Stepan, Vladimir, and Pavel have died (the latter is "comforted" by the unctuous Porphyry, but has enough life in him to shout from his deathbed, "Go away, you bloodsucker!"), Porphyry comes alive, and takes control of the estate.

Porphyry is Shchedrin's great creation. His vivacity as a character proceeds, in part, from a paradox, which is that he is interesting in proportion to his banality. Traditionally, the great fictional hypocrites are generally interesting as liars are interesting. But Porphyry does not really lie to himself, for the truth is nowhere to be found in his world. He speaks the "truths" (as he sees them) that are all around him, and they are the most dismal, banal, lying platitudes. Shchedrin is explicit about this at one point. The hypocrites of French drama, he writes, are "conscious hypocrites, that is, they know it themselves and are aware that other people know it too." Porphyry, he writes, "was a hypocrite of a purely Russian sort, that is, simply a man devoid of all moral standards, knowing no truth other than the copy-book precepts. He was pettifogging, deceitful, loquacious, boundlessly ignorant, and afraid of the devil. All these qualities are merely negative and can supply no stable material for real hypocrisy."

Porphyry grinds down his mother and his servants with endless banalities. His usual technique is to invoke God: "What would God say?" His sure idea of God's providence is used to justify his cruelty, his swindling, his meanness, and his theft. There is a vivid and comic scene as his brother Pavel is dying. Porphyry arrives in a coach-and-four; immediately his mother thinks to herself, "The Fox must have scented a carcass." Porphyry enters the house with his two sons, Volodenka and Petenka (Volodenka mimicking his father's pieties, "folding his hands, rolling his eyes and moving his lips"). Seeing his mother unhappy, Porphyry says to her: "You are despondent, I see! It's wrong, dear! Oh, it's very wrong! You should ask yourself, 'And what would God say to that?' Why, He would say, 'Here I arrange everything for the best in My wisdom, and she repines!'" He continues:

> As a brother—I am grieved. More than once, in fact, I may have wept. I am grieving over my brother, grieving deeply. . . . I shed tears, but then I think: "And what about God? Doesn't God know better than we do?" One considers this and feels cheered. That's what everyone ought to do. . . . Look at me. See how well I'm bearing up!

Still, Porphyry is afraid. He spends much of his time crossing himself, or praying before his icons. In true Golovlyov fashion, he prays not for anything positive, but negatively, to be saved from the devil. (It is a nice implicit joke that Porphyry is afraid of the devil but is in fact the devil.) "He could go on praying and performing all the necessary movements, and at the same time be looking out of the window to see if anyone went to the cellar without permission." Porphyry uses religious platitudes to protect himself from anything that would threaten his survival; religious hypocrisy is his moral camouflage.

One of the most horrifying events in the novel occurs when Porphyry's son Petenka comes home to beg for money. He has gambled away three thousand rubles belonging to his regiment, and if he cannot pay them back, he will be sent off to Siberia. Petenka enters his father's study; Porphyry is kneeling, with uplifted arms. He keeps his son waiting for half an hour on purpose, and when Petenka finally explains that he has lost money, Porphyry replies, "amiably": "Well, return it!" When Petenka tells him that he doesn't have that kind of money, Porphyry warns him not to "mix me up in your dirty affairs. Let us go and have breakfast instead. We'll drink tea and sit quietly and perhaps talk of something, only, for Christ's sake, not this." Bitterly, Petenka says to his father, "I am the only son you have left," and his father replies: "God took from Job all he had, my dear, and yet he did not repine, but only said, 'God has given, God has taken away—God's will be done.' So that's the way, my boy."

Hypocrisy is a familiar subject in Russian literature—Gogol's landowners, Dostoevsky's governors, Chekhov's doctor in "Ward 6"—and within it, religious hypocrisy has a special place. The traditional hypocrite may, in his extremism, unwittingly strengthen the visible moral code. But religion, which is itself an extremism, must be weakened by the hypocrite's misuse of it. Religion, after all, unlike ordinary morality, is a devotion—one professes it—so the Christian hypocrite commits an enhanced crime: hypocrisy about which one should certainly not be hypocritical. Thus he may awaken in people the conclusion that religion is itself a hypocrisy: since religion is itself already a profession of morality, it may seem that religion is the source of its hypocritical profession.

Morality is misused by the traditional hypocrite; but religion is only used by the religious hypocrite. Heresy lurks in the distinction. Outside Russian literature, Fielding's Parson Adams, though a benign creature, tends to discredit the Christianity which enables his hypocrisy. And Stendhal, depicting the hypocritical priests of *The Red and the Black*, means to provoke heresy. So too, in a gentler way, does Chekhov, the son of a terrible religious hypocrite, when, in his story "In the Ravine," he makes fun of a priest who pompously comforts a woman who has just lost her baby while pointing at her with "a fork with a pickled mushroom at the end."

When he began to write *The Golovlyov Family*, in the latter half of the 1870s, Shchedrin, who was known as Russia's greatest satirist, had already mocked religious hypocrisy in his *Fables*, a collection of Aesopian tales about feeble governors, greedy landowners, imbecilic bureaucrats, and cruel priests. In "A Village Fire," a widow loses her only son to the flames, and the priest, like Porphyry, accuses her of grieving too much. "Why this plaint?" he asks her, "with kindly reproach." The priest tells her the story of Job and reminds her that Job did not complain, "but still more loved the Lord who had created him." Later in the story, when the daughter of the village's landowner tells her mother of the widow's suffering, the landowner, like Porphyry, invokes destiny: "It's dreadful for her; but how worked up you are, Vera! . . . That will never do, my love. There's a Purpose in all things—we must always remember!"

At times *The Golovlyov Family* seems less a novel than a satirical onslaught. Its relentlessness has the exhaustiveness not of a search for the truth so much as the prosecution of a case. Its characters are vivid blots of essence, carriers of the same single vice. Indeed, Shchedrin would seem to enjoy shocking the reader by annulling the novel's traditional task, that of the patient exploration, and elucidation, of private motives and reasons as they are played out in relation to a common condition. Instead, he gives us his sealed monsters, people whom we cannot explore since they are shut off from the moral world. Shchedrin knows how terrible, how—given the conventions of the novel—shocking it is to witness Stepan's homecoming, which is a cruel inversion of the parable of the Prodigal Son: "All understood that the man before them was an unloved son who had come to the place he hated, that he had come for good and that his only escape from it would be to be carried, feet foremost, to the churchyard. And all felt both sorry for him and uneasy." All except Stepan's mother, of course.

Shchedrin knows that it is both a kind of affront to decency and to the decency of the novel itself to present a family reunion in such inhuman terms, and his narration, at points throughout the book, registers the offense. Usually, Shchedrin breaks in to tell us what we should think about each character, acting as an omniscient satirist. But at other times, he writes as if from one of the character's minds. When Stepan returns, Arina, Pavel, and Porphyry hold a family conference to discuss his fate. Arina tells Porphyry and Pavel that she has decided to allow Stepan the meanest of allowances. Shchedrin writes: "Although Porphyry Vladimiritch had refused to act as a judge, he was so struck by his mother's generosity that he felt it his duty to point out to her the dangerous consequences to which the proposed measure might lead." Since the reader can see that there is nothing "generous" about Arina, the novel's narration, at this point, is ironic, affecting to think of Arina as Porphyry might think of his mother. Yet we know that Porphyry can never be trusted, and that Porphyry never thinks well of anyone. What does it mean, then, to be told that he thought his mother generous? Is it possible that the moral sense has been so polluted in Porphyry that, even though he hates his mother, he credits his own hypocritical lies, his own devious fawning and playacting, and actually believes his mother to be generous at this moment? Or, more simply, is it just that Porphyry truly thinks that Arina's terms are too good for Stepan, that, in effect, Porphyry hates his brother more than his mother? Shchedrin's devilish twist is that he has left us alone: we do not know.

This technique, antinovelistic in its essence, nonetheless grants Shchedrin a peculiar novelistic power of his own. He uses it to bring us closer to the characters, letting us, if only for a minute, inhabit the wilderness of their souls. The method is especially effective when used with Porphyry, for we are made to share in his self-deceptions. Here Shchedrin's narration is genuinely "unreliable," and unreliable about an already unreliable man. At one devastating moment in the novel, Shchedrin writes of Porphyry: "He had lost all connections with the outside world. He received no books, no newspapers, no letters. One of his sons, Volodenka, had committed suicide; to his other son, Petenka, he wrote very little, and only when he sent him money." The reader starts at this: the last time Volodenka was mentioned by Shchedrin, he was a little boy, mimicking his father. This is the first time we have heard anything about his committing suicide. But again, if we see the sentence as, in effect, issuing from Porphyry's mind, it is just the heartless way that he would think of his dead son—as an unimportant memory, hardly worth mentioning.

The closer Shchedrin brings us to Porphyry, the more unknowable he actually becomes. In this sense, Porphyry is a modernist prototype: the character who lacks an audience, the alienated actor. The hypocrite who does not know he is one, and can never really be told that he is one by anyone around him, is something of a revolutionary fictional character, for he has no "true" knowable self, no "stable ego," to use D. H. Lawrence's phrase. Around the turn of the twentieth century, Knut Hamsun, a novelist strongly influenced by Dostoevsky and the Russian novel, would invent a new kind of character: the lunatic heroes of his novels *Hunger* and *Mysteries* go around telling falsely incriminating stories about themselves and acting badly when they have no obvious reason to. It is difficult to know when they are lying and not lying, and impossible to understand their motives. They too are unknowable, even though they are, in a sense, antihypocrites, so deeply in revolt against the pieties of Lutheranism that they have become parodically impious. They broadcast their self-invented sinfulness in the streets, though no one is really listening. The line from Dostoevsky, through Shchedrin, and on to Hamsun, is visible. In this regard, *The Golovlyov Family*, this strange, raucous book, whose characters both suffer from and aspire to the condition of nothingness, a book which is at times broad satire, at times Gothic horror, and at times an antinovel, becomes more modern the older it gets.

Elizabeth Hardwick on

THE UNPOSSESSED

BY TESS SLESINGER

THE UNPOSSESSED is a daring, unique fiction, a wild, crowded comedy set in New York City in the 1930s. The inchoate, irrational, addictive metropolis, ever clamoring, brawling between its two somehow sluggish rivers, is a challenge to its citizens and to the novelist's art. In the end, people gather with their own kind, as they do in the towns with the right side to live in and the wrong side, with Baptists and Catholics, girls brought up for the Junior League and others to become plump, nice ladies taking covered dishes to the Oddfellows picnic. Manhattan, ever a proper symbol of an immigrant nation, lives in the daytime by "immigrants" from the boroughs who come in to build the skyscrapers, paint the walls, caulk the leaking pipes, drive the cabs; it is also the dream site of travelers from Alabama, Illinois, or Michigan with the longing of their specialized ambition to go on the stage, master the Steinway grand, paint pictures, or write stories for *The New Yorker*.

The city is, as it must be, a nest of enclaves in the surrounding smother. *The Unpossessed* looks with a

ELIZABETH HARDWICK

subversive eye on a disorderly, self-appointed group: intellectuals, critical of society's arrangements and very critical of each other. It is the 1930s and the reign, you might call it, of the left; of well-to-do Greenwich Village friends of the workers striking in Detroit and of the woebegone, cotton-picking sharecroppers of the South. Above all, the echoes from the "classless" society in Russia, the proles sending the feckless aristocrats to Paris, aroused in intellectual circles here a sort of conversational communism.

The Unpossessed is a kindly act of intellectual friendship written by a sensibility formed by the period and yet almost helplessly alert to the follies of a programmatic "free love" and the knots and tangles of parlor radicalism. Tess Slesinger, the author, was born in New York, the daughter of a non-practicing Jewish family. Her father, Hungarian by birth, attended City College but after marriage went into the garment business owned by his wife's family, the Singers. The garment business seems to be almost foreordained in the history of Jews in the city and not more on the dot than the fact of the author's mother, early education interrupted to work in the family business, ending up, after night classes, and a spell with Erich Fromm and Karen Horney, as a lay analyst and along the way taking part in the beginning of the New School for Social Research.

Tess Slesinger attended the progressive school, Ethical Culture, Swarthmore College, and the Columbia School

124

of Journalism. She married Herbert Solow, a man about town in intellectual circles, who was on the staff of the *Menorah Journal* and, much later, like the progression of so many radicals, on the staff of *Fortune* magazine. By way of the *Menorah Journal*, it was the world of Elliot Cohen, Clifton Fadiman, and Lionel Trilling that this young woman, at the age of twenty-three, more gifted than any in the group except Trilling, inhabited in her fashion. She published short stories and, in 1934, her only novel, *The Unpossessed*; was divorced from Solow, and went to Hollywood. There she married Frank Davis, a producer, had two children, a son and a daughter, worked on successful screenplays, and died at the age of thirty-nine. A crowded life indeed and far more than a footnote in American literature.

The Unpossessed is overflowing with "characters": grocers, cabbies, waiters passing through the landscape briefly, but each there in his own singular skin. And of course the characters of fiction with their wives, their money or lack of it, their careers, their presentation of themselves in battle with the self they fear from knowing it far too well. Miles Flinders, a New Englander surviving the terrible trips to the woodshed for punishment by Uncle Dan and yet masochistically suffering from his own knowledge that his sins were greater than those Uncle Dan was thrashing. His "balmy" wife Margaret, kind, intelligent, wishing to please and for that reason somewhat a burden to Miles.

Jeffrey Blake, a second-rate novelist and master forni-
cator, is first seen expertly mixing cocktails in the
kitchen with the help of Margaret Flinders while Miles,
from his unhappy childhood a believer in economic de-
terminism, is in the next room with Jeffrey's wife,
Norah, explaining that economic conditions control all,
even marriage. Meanwhile, Jeffrey is flinging himself,
as if obliged to do so, against Margaret and saying, "Are
you never going to throw away your bourgeois notions,
are we always condemned to sin against ourselves and
our desire. . . ."

Bruno Leonard, of German Jewish origin, had been in
college with Jeffrey Blake and Miles Flinders, and now
in New York they are planning, somewhat murkily, to
put out a magazine. Throughout the drunken pages, the
floating ship of private life sails in the waters of the historical moment: the Depression, apple sellers in the
street, the Scottsboro boys on trial, Walter Damrosch
concerts, the plays of Eugene O'Neill, about which Miles
says, "My Uncle Daniel would have sneered at 'Beyond
the Horizon'; even my father would have walked out
on it—staggered out, to the nearest saloon."

The Magazine, instrument of arcane propaganda and
personal identity for the little band of pinkos, figures
in the hopes like a valuable visitor one hasn't the money
to entertain with a suitable feast. Jeffrey has somehow
learned of a certain Comrade Fisher who might have his
hand in the pocket of the Party. Comrade Fisher turns

out to be a bulky woman, whose name is Ruthie. Ruthie is a sloganeering geyser who, nevertheless, has some poignant items on her résumé. She has actually spent a night in jail, has been the lover of one Comrade Turner, a mill worker who led a famous strike. Jeffrey, seeking his own claim as a revolutionary fit for international celebrity, will end up in bed with Comrade Ruthie, homely as she is, and through her tired flesh experience a sort of mystical transformation:

> He lay and listened peacefully to the revolutionary bedtime story, his hands at rest on her head as though her story, her former loves, the spirit of Comrade Turner, the spirit of the strike itself, passed through her and into his fingers. . . . He was Comrade Turner lying with Comrade Fisher in his arms. . . . He was the raw-boned mill worker who led the strike. He was the many mill-hands singing the International. . . . Gratitude toward Comrade Fisher overwhelmed him like love. He threw off the hot counterpane and made love to Comrade Fisher, Comrade Turner's Comrade Fisher, under Comrade Lenin's sightless eyes.

There is indeed no financial advantage to Ruthie, who has after an uncomfortable trip to the Soviet Union become a Trotskyite. But there is money, big money, elsewhere in the Middleton family, parents of one of

Bruno's students at the university where he teaches in a lackadaisical manner that enchants the young with their own revolt against the unholy powers of the school administration and the capitalist tyranny of the society they live in.

Mrs. Middleton, along the way seduced by the importunate Jeffrey, will give an evening party, a fund-raiser for the Hunger March gathering in Washington and for the Magazine. Radicals, rich friends, antiques mostly, of "old New York" society, the butler, the band, the buffet table laden with ham, turkey, sturgeon, caviar, and from a celestial bakery a pastry in the shape of the Capitol in Washington. Conversation is picked up, lost, returned to once more; syllables of comment, private matters between old acquaintances resurrected and cast into the party din.

The band leader is a melancholy, failed classical composer doomed to ballads and fox trots and oldies for a tone-deaf audience. The poor man, remembering his ambitious days, chooses to play the Allegro (Spring) from his rejected "Symphony of the Seasons."

"Beethoven, isn't it?" said a Miss Hobson. Around her, there is talk of horses, one named Minerva. "You liked that blind-in-one-eye, spavined, consumptive creature with a rotten gallop like a Ford, *wh-why*!" Mrs. Stanhope whinnied in her horror. "You know it's possible it's Brahms," said Mr. Terrill suddenly. The band leader is requested to leave off and play "After the Ball

Was Over." "Thank God for that," Mr. Terrill whispered. "I never really cared for Debussy anyhow." The bits of musical and horse appreciation are scattered over many pages, drifting in and out in the crowded rooms.

There is comment in a similar spread about a modest Negro gentleman, Graham Hatcher, invited in a period of one for every party to liven things up. It is felt he must "represent" something: "in musical comedy perhaps." "I wonder," said Ruthie Fisher, "if he might not be the communist candidate for vice-president; he must be *somebody*." Mr. Hatcher wearily smiles and says he doesn't represent anything, but a guest will be heard saying he might be the house detective. The host, Mr. Middleton, name of Al, makes club-man, Wall Street jokes throughout the evening and decides that the courteous black gentleman might have "some pullman porter blood." Or, from another part of the room, "Ooooh, I wonder could he be Paul Robeson." At last, Mr. Hatcher, standing about dressed in his singular complexion: "I am *not* the entertainment," he exploded, "God damn it, I am Vice President of the C.F.S.U.S.—The Colored Folks' Social Uplift Society." To a Mr. Ballister who could hear and to Miss Ballister who couldn't it is explained that the C.F.S.U.S. must be some little magazine the colored folks are starting.

In the moil, a Mrs. Fancher enters to be identified for the unknowing outsiders by the knowing Al: "Lady entering in pearls is our first prison-widow. Husband embezzled. Got five years. Damn shame. Best card player I ever knew." In the staccato brilliance of the party scene more than two dozen voices and human shapes appear in a raucous mingling—not anonymous names on a list but creations distinct and placed in the social order. Miss Bee Powell, a Daughter of the Confederacy with "violet eyes framed in Junior League eyelashes"; Mrs. Stanhope, the horsewoman who never leaves the paddock; Mr. Crawford, "who fell short of being an English lord only by birth and a monocle," will say "jolly, jolly" at every turn; the butler, of uncertain lineage, has by his station transmogrified into a Republican who would "feed beggars at the backdoor and throw away the rag with which he wiped their crumbs." The pages have the reckless exuberance of the open bar, the dance floor, the plentiful harvest of the buffet table, the tribal company, each in its vanity, language, armor, and folly.

Bruno will be called upon to give a fund-raising speech for the Magazine and, dead-drunk, will fall into a long, self-destructive rant of misplaced irony that only an intellectual could excavate from his rattled brain:

> "Are we as intellectuals going to remain sitting on the fence, watching Christian Science fight with Freud? are we going to twiddle our thumbs and stew in our juices while the world is on the breadlines, the redlines, the deadlines? . . ." He tottered, swayed. . . . He recovered and straightened,

bowed with a homosexual Tammany smile.... "The answer is: 'WE ARE.'" The laugh broke out, relieved, the merry cocktail laugh, the self-indulgent, self-effulgent upper-class champagne laugh....

"But comrades! need I tell you ... we must have competent defeatist leadership ... in short we are bastards, foundlings, phonys, the unpossessed and unpossessing of the world, the real minority...."

The final chapter shifts to Margaret and Miles Flinders and to the Greenway Maternity Home where Margaret has gone for an abortion or for treatment after having had one. Miles, when the time came, could not face the diapers drying on the radiator, the convulsive change a baby would make in their lives, although he phrased the drastic moment as fear of going "soft" and "bourgeois." It's a downward slide, this last chapter, a haunting return to private life. And again composed in a tornado of broken dialogue among the women having babies, one born dead and another having her fourth, a girl, when what was wanted was a boy after three girls.

The composition will center on a huge basket of fruit, now scarcely touched, which Margaret will forlornly offer to her ward companions and to the cabdriver taking her home. "Missis Butter, won't you?" No, Missis Butter has plenty of fruit of her own. "Missis Wiggam, wouldn't you?" No, can't hold acids after a baby. To the cabdriver: "You must have a peach"; but "Mr. Strite had never cared for peaches; the skin got in his teeth." And no, he wouldn't have an apple, "must be getting on uptown." Mr. Strite at last accepts a pear, " 'For luck,' he said, managing an excellent American smile." In an unexpected, deftly managed change of tone, the rejected basket of fruit becomes the rejected baby—a symbol, if you like.

The Unpossessed, noticeable indeed, was widely noticed when it appeared. The reviews were more benign in the traditional press than in *The New Masses*, or especially in *The Daily Worker*. Subversives are ever alert to traitors in their own ranks; traitors by way of style are a subtle threat to content, as even the uncultivated Stalin understood. It has been suggested that Virginia Woolf and Katherine Mansfield may have been models for Tess Slesinger. Perhaps, but their art is more serene and controlled than the fractured eloquence of the polyphonic pages of *The Unpossessed*, interestingly dedicated: *to my contemporaries*.

Lydia Davis on

THE LIFE OF HENRY BRULARD

BY STENDHAL

THE OTHER day I was listening to a program about astronomy on the radio, and in the space of about half an hour I learned at least five or six startling things, among them: that most meteors are no larger than a raisin; that a meteor the size of a grape would light up the entire sky as it descended; that if we could see him, a person poised on the edge of a black hole would appear, from the vantage point of the earth, to hover there indefinitely, frozen in time, whereas from the vantage point of the black hole itself he would be swallowed up instantly. Some of this was hard for me to understand, and while I was still agog with it, along came the next and most disturbing comment, one concerning the nature of time: there is, they said, a good deal of evidence suggesting that at the deepest level of reality, time as we are accustomed to imagine it does not actually exist, that we live in an eternal present.

If I can comprehend it at all, this idea is not a very comfortable one. I would prefer to think of objective time as an unbroken stream of equal intervals stretching infinitely far back and far forward; then I may peaceably watch subjective time as it defies measurement by behaving in its usual capricious, elastic, elusive manner, shrinking and expanding unexpectedly or collapsing in on itself. And this was my habit of thought before I heard the radio program and while I was engrossed in reading Stendhal's *Life of Henry Brulard*. For time is very much one of the subjects of this *Life*, which remarkably transfigures or transcends it, as Stendhal looks back at his past and speaks forward in time to his readers of the future, but also, by his manner of writing, brings those readers into what now seems to me, after the radio program, to be an eternal present.

Stendhal wrote this strangely fragmented, digressive, and yet beautifully structured pseudonymous memoir in four quick months over the winter of 1835–1836. He had written *The Red and the Black* five years earlier, in 1830; and he was to write *The Charterhouse of Parma* (another quick book, occupying the seven weeks from early November to late December) less than two years later, in 1838. At the age of fifty-three, he is looking back at the first seventeen years of his life, at the events of what we would call—and what he would recognize as—his "formative" years and subjecting them to a close examination and analysis "so as to work out what sort of man I have been."

Yet he is also looking ahead, contemplating and occasionally addressing the readers who will pick up his book in 1880, readers who, he thinks, may be more sympathetic to him than his contemporaries—though just as often, he frets that they will be intolerably bored by the minutiae of his life. "I have no doubt had great pleasure from writing this past hour, and from trying to describe my feelings of the time *exactly as they were*," he says, "but who on earth will be brave enough to go deeply into it, to read this excessive heap of *I*s and *me*s?"

He occasionally, even, looks beyond the readers of 1880 to those of 1900, 1935, and, surprisingly, our own 2000. He is not sure, he says, if the reader of the future will still be familiar with *Les Liaisons dangereuses* by Choderlos de Laclos—yes, we still know it, we would like to answer him. He believes the reader of 1900 and one hundred years later will certainly have a more enlightened understanding of Racine. Well, there we would probably disappoint him.

Whenever we read a book, of course, time, in a sense, collapses: we feel we are reading in the same moment the writer is writing, or that we cause him to speak, and as he speaks we hear him—there is no interval; and the converse, that we have only to stop reading for a moment, and he stops speaking. What immediate authority the handwritten message of a dead parent still has! And it is true that a reader is the necessary completion of the act of writing. Yet Stendhal's *Life*, more than most, jumps beyond the bounds of its time and tradition, speaks across nearly two centuries in an intensely personal voice.

How does it achieve such immediacy? And why is this minutely detailed tabulation by this irascible grumbler so appealing?

Certainly it shares some of the qualities of other eccentric autobiographical works that continue to strike us as fresh and new despite the passage of time (if time does indeed pass): Kafka's *Letter to His Father*, Cyril Connolly's *The Unquiet Grave*, J. R. Ackerley's *Hindoo Holiday*, Gertrude Stein's *Autobiography of Alice B. Toklas*, *Roland Barthes by Roland Barthes*, Rousseau's *Confessions*, Theresa Hak Kyung Cha's *Dictée*, Michel Leiris's *Rules of the Game*. For one thing, the style of *The Life of Henry Brulard* is plain and straightforward, conversational and direct. For another, it is full of keenly observed and striking detail—a room so cold the ink freezes on the tip of the pen, a dying man carried home on a ladder, clothes "smelling of the makers."

It is written with passion. Stendhal, like the narrator of a Thomas Bernhard novel, is terribly attached to his every feeling. He is just as furious today (at the time of his writing and our reading) as he was at age fourteen, when his greatest love was mathematics ("I fancy I said to myself: '*true or false, mathematics will get me out of Grenoble*, out of this mire that turns my stomach' ") and he was endlessly frustrated by the complacency and hypocrisy of his teachers: what a shock, he says, "when I realized that no one could explain to me how it is that a minus times a minus equals a plus $(- \times - = +)$!" Further rage when no one will resolve another puzzle: is it or is it not true that parallel lines, when produced to infinity, will eventually meet?

Clear-eyed about his good points and bad, Stendhal aims for accuracy ("I am witty no more than once a week and then only for five minutes," he tells us), and what a complex and interesting person emerges from this self-examination. Stubborn, opinionated, cantankerous, yet brilliant, minutely observant, and appealingly fallible. Not an easy friend; someone in whose company one would be always on edge—he would be sure to pounce on any sign of fatuousness or mental sloth. Intellectually ambitious, and not merely concerning literature and politics: he still thinks he ought to study worms and beetles—"which nauseate me"—as he had intended to do while he was a soldier fighting under Napoleon.

He has much to say about memory because he is relying entirely on that unreliable faculty in his re-creation of his early years. There is a great deal, he tells us, that he had forgotten until the present moment of writing: things come back to him that he has not thought of for decades. He often says that a certain memory is obscured because of the great emotion he experienced at the time: the emotion wiped out the memory. He points out, further, that if he remembers this much of an event, he has also forgotten a great deal more, but that if he were to begin supplementing the truth with his imagination, he would be writing a novel and not a memoir. "I protest once again that I don't claim to be describing things in themselves, but only their effect on me."

Yet *The Life of Henry Brulard* has several even more unusual features. For one thing, there are the *aide-memoire* sketches, nearly two hundred of them, thin, spidery diagrams with scribbled explanations showing where young Stendhal was positioned in relation to others, in a room or on a mountainside, in a street or a square ("I clouted him with all my might at O"), and these sketches, minimal, crabbed, and repetitious as they are, oddly enough make his memories more real to us too.

For another, there is his abiding and multilayered pretense at self-concealment. He not only refers to himself at points as a certain overly loquacious "Dominique," but more significantly titles the book (on the title-pages of several sections of the manuscript) as *Life of Henry Brulard written by himself* and then describes it, for the benefit of "Messrs of the police," not as an autobiography but as a novel in imitation of the very bland and innocent *Vicar of Wakefield*. Now, all the layers of the self-concealment are quite transparent: he is not Henry Brulard, he is not writing a novel, and this book does not in any obvious way resemble Goldsmith's tale. It seems unlikely that he is making a serious effort to protect himself, or even that this is merely a sustained joke. It seems more likely that the man we obligingly refer to as

Stendhal, but who was of course actually Henri Beyle, and who made a habit of adopting a variety of pseudonyms in his published writings, must have been more comfortable erecting a screen of fiction behind which he could give himself permission to write with utter sincerity. There is in fact a wonderful moment well into the book where the real and the fictional names are forcibly melded in an act of sheer impudence, when Stendhal refers to "the five letters: B,R,U,L,A,R,D, that form my name."

And then, the book appears to be unfinished. Certainly it is unusually rough. Passages of expansive, fully developed narrative will be followed by a succession of terse one-sentence paragraphs, fleeting afterthoughts, qualifications, or digressions inspired by his narration—and perhaps such brief paragraphs are a perfect representation of the disconnected way in which our thoughts sometimes move. Stendhal has left blank spaces in the text where he has forgotten a name or can't think of the right adjective. He has abbreviated words freely, motivated sometimes by haste and sometimes by (he says) a fear of censorship. He includes occasional cryptic private references and secret codes. He inserts reminders to himself throughout the text, usually in the margins, or corrects errors as he goes along (below a diagram: "Entrance steps or rather no entrance steps"). He repeats himself, twice asserting, for instance, that the only passions that have remained with him throughout his life

seven drafts of "Testaments" bequeathing the manuscript to a host of possible publishers, including the
bookseller Levavasseur, with instructions to publish it
fifteen years after Stendhal's death with all the women's
names changed and none of the men's.)

Why is the fragmented, the rough, sometimes so
much more inviting than the seamless, the polished?
Because we are closer to the moment of creation?
("Handwriting," he notes in a margin. "This is how I
write when my thoughts are treading on my heels. . . .")
Because we are intimate witnesses to the formulation of
the thought? Inside the experience of the writer instead
of outside? Because we are closer to the evolution by
which an event of the past, long forgotten—though evidently somewhere present in the brain cells of the
writer—is reawakened, reimagined, re-presented, put
into words? ("My heart is pounding still as I write this
thirty-six years later. I abandon my paper, I wander
round my room and I come back to writing.") As though
we were taking part ourselves, involved in and identify-
ing with the action, the action being in this case the re-
creation and understanding of a life?

Perhaps, too, a work that comes to us so fresh, so raw,
from the writer's mind is more exciting because we see
how precarious is the writer's control—the material is
almost more powerful than he is. As Stendhal himself
says, it was the material—his ideas, his memories—that
commanded him, not some "literary ideal." And so it is

a work that changes as he writes it, that is full of his own discovery as he goes along; and for his own purposes, and to our delight, he notes the elaboration of this memoir even as he writes it.

At one point in his narration Stendhal refers casually to a moment later in his life when he was in mortal danger: alone in a Silesian field, he saw coming towards him a company of Cossacks. He does not go on to tell us what happened next. I wondered, as I continued reading, whether he was merely being artful and would satisfy my curiosity before the book ended. I suspected he would not, and he did not. His intention in the book, after all, is not to tell a dramatic story. Yet a different, and greater, drama unfolds as we read, because of the constant double surprise: being alongside him as he works, rather than being handed the result of a later revision, we surprise him in the very act of writing even as he surprises himself in the act of remembering and understanding. And so we are privileged to watch what is really the very dramatic moment, enacted again and again, of the unremembered or half-remembered being fully brought to mind, the unformed being formed, the internal becoming external, the private becoming public.

THE PILGRIM HAWK

BY GLENWAY WESCOTT

WE MAY consider Glenway Wescott's *The Pilgrim Hawk* to be a short novel or a long novella, but whatever we choose to call it, it is exactly as long as it needs to be. It is murderously precise and succinct. It contains, in its 108 pages, more levels and layers of experience than many books five times its length.

The book centers on various overlapping triangles among a group of beings who are mostly, but not exclusively, human. It takes place during a single summer afternoon in the late 1920s in a French country house, where Alexandra Henry, the young American heiress who owns it, is entertaining an American house guest named Alwyn Tower, the book's narrator. On this particular afternoon Alexandra and Tower are visited by the Cullens, a wealthy Irish couple who, in their on-going and rather aimless travels, are en route to Budapest in a Daimler, driven by their young chauffeur. Larry Cullen is, or at least appears to be, the very image of the hale, silly aristocrat. His wife, Madeleine, is an aging beauty who has spent her marriage dragging her husband through one rough devotion after another, most of them

143

MICHAEL CUNNINGHAM

involving radical Irish politics or the killing of some wild animal, and who appears at the château with her latest enthusiasm, a hawk she is training to hunt. She has named the hawk Lucy, after the Walter Scott and Donizetti heroine, and she wears it perched on her wrist like a sacred jewel.

At the same time a parallel story transpires in the kitchen, involving Ricketts, the chauffeur, and Alexandra's servants, Jean and Eva, a husband and wife from Morocco. These seven characters—eight if we include the hawk, and we must include the hawk—are the novel's entire population. From this small cast of characters, in the course of what should be an innocuous interlude of cocktails and dinner, Wescott summons a series of revelations that doesn't stop until the book's ambiguous, quietly lethal last lines.

Beyond that, I see no point in a detailed synopsis. Suffice it to say that *The Pilgrim Hawk* is an endlessly intricate meditation on freedom versus captivity and passion versus peace, among other subjects; and that in terms of character and event it is strung throughout with little bombs, some of which explode on contact, some considerably later. Rendered geometrically, the novel's structure might resemble a series of intersecting triangles canted at various angles in space, irregular but perfect, in the way of quartz crystals. With its single bucolic setting and the desperate, strangling wit and manners of its most prominent characters, it owes a good

144

deal to Chekhov. Wescott shares with Chekhov an insistence that the enormous is amply contained within the small; that the ingredients of tragedy can be found in abundance among genteel, indolent people passing an afternoon together in a parlor and a garden.

All that occurs in *The Pilgrim Hawk* takes place within the borders of this miniature world. The action does not extend beyond the house and grounds—even the book's one incident of physical violence takes place outside our range of vision. The whole story could be presented on stage with almost no alterations. Its static quality is, however, by no means accidental. The narrative is restricted in the way that the bird (and the people) are confined. As the story progresses we learn that every domesticated hawk has been captured in the wild, since hawks do not mate or breed in captivity. "They never get over being wild," as Mrs. Cullen says, and though trained hawks could always choose to fly away when hunting, they do not, she explains, because in captivity "it's a better life, more food and more fun."

Some readers may groan inwardly, as I did, when I first read about the hawk. Oh, I thought, a symbol. And the hawk is, of course, a symbol—hawks are members of a small category of creatures and objects that can't be anything but symbols when they appear in books. However, if novelists are determined, as they should be, to write about everything in the world, it is just as important to find new life in the old images as it is to invent new ones. Wescott knew what he was up against, what sort of portentousness he flirted with, and it is a measure of his talent that he was able not only to fully engage what might be implied by such a stubbornly meaningful image but also to create a hawk that is, apart from its larger meaning, an entirely convincing, integral member of the story. Wescott was a man who had *looked* at hawks:

> [The hawk's] body was as long as her mistress's arm; the wing feathers in repose a little too long, slung across her back like a folded tent.... Her luxurious breast was white, with little tabs or tassels of chestnut. Out of tasseled pantaloons her legs came down straight to the perch with no apparent flesh on them, enameled a greenish yellow.
>
> But her chief beauty was that of expression. It was like a little flame; it caught and compelled your attention like that, although it did not flicker and there was nothing bright about it nor any warmth in it. It is a look that men sometimes have; men of great energy, whose appetite or vocation has kept them absorbed every instant all their lives. They may be good men but they are often mistaken for evil men, and vice versa. In Lucy's case it appeared chiefly in her eyes, not black but funereally brown, and extravagantly large, set deep in her flattened head.

The hawk's wonderfully drawn wildness—its profound otherness—slices like a razor through the world
of indolent expatriate luxury in which the book is set,
some years before the Second World War, which will not
only send Alwyn Tower and Alexandra Henry fleeing
back to America but will extinguish a certain lazy, genteel optimism; a belief in the relative sanctity of hedges
and lawns as well as a more general belief in our collec-
tive ability to select and enforce happy endings. The
book declares itself at the start to be set in a less difficult
past; to be both lit and obscured by wistfulness. We
learn, through Mrs. Cullen, that only captive hawks
have any chance of living out their natural spans—in the
wild they always die of starvation, when they grow too
old to hunt—and as we read we pick up stray fragments
about the loneliness and failure that await some of the
characters as certainly as war awaits the world in which
they live. Most significantly we receive, in the opening
line, an offhand and all but invisible reference to what
the future holds for Tower and Alexandra, though we are
not permitted to understand what their futures imply
until we reach the story's end.

Every character proves, by the book's close, to be
more than he or she first seemed to be, just as every
relationship turns out to be far more complex and
perverse than we might have imagined at the outset.
This is most conspicuously true of the Cullens, whom
we meet as relatively standard-issue eccentrics, two of

the wealthy, outdoorsy people Alexandra has coped with all her privileged life, "self-centered but without any introspection, strenuous but emotionally idle." By the end of the quietly calamitous afternoon, superficial Cullen is revealed as a tragic and potentially dangerous figure, driven to extremes by a jealousy broad and deep enough to include a bird. Mrs. Cullen metamorphoses from a chilly matron into a rough, wild Irish girl grown old and, finally, into something like an Amazon. As she tries to retrieve the hawk after it has escaped we see that

> that French or Italian footwear of hers with three-inch heels not only incapacitated her but flattered her, and disguised her. Now her breasts seemed lower on her torso, out of the way of her nervous arms. Her hips were wide and her back powerful, with that curve from the shoulder blades to the head which you see in the nudes of Ingres. She walked with her legs well apart, one padding footfall after another, as impossible to trip up as a cat.

The book treats the parallel drama among Jean, Eva, and Ricketts as peripheral—they live in the novel as they live in the households of Alexandra and the Cullens: in cars and kitchens, out of the way. They are, of course, captives themselves, and they matter more or less the way wild pets matter: as curiosities, as sources of trouble, and, more obscurely, as subjugated invaders from a realm of frighteningly rampant desires. Wescott chose to depict his vanishing world from the point of view of those who are served, and to let the servers remain as obscure to the reader as they are to their keepers. The story immerses us not only in a world but in a particular way of living in that world. Jean, Eva, and the chauffeur, like the titular hawk, play crucial roles in the stories of the wealthy but exist in a world of their own as well. One imagines they pass through this novel while living out an unwritten novel of their own, one in which they are the central figures, and the commotion created by those people in the parlor is important but secondary.

At the center of the story, omnipresent but also concealed, is Alwyn Tower himself, and he proves to be the darkest and most surprising figure of all. Tower lives within the confines of his own domesticity more or less as the hawk does, for similar reasons—it's a better life, more food and more fun—and probably at similar cost, though Wescott is too subtle to offer a mere plea, in narrative form, for freedom over captivity. Tower is not yet old but is no longer young. He is trying, and failing, to write novels, and he has been in love twice, though we learn nothing of the particulars in either case. (In one of the book's many symmetries we are told that trained hawks can only tolerate two consecutive unsuccessful strikes before they despair and fly away, to a freedom that will eventually starve them to death.) Tower is essentially an engine of perception, of exquisitely cruel and precise judgments. Although he has failed at writing he is, in a sense, the very embodiment of the novelist, who must of necessity see more than his characters see, know more about them than they can know about themselves. If this is a requisite virtue in a novelist, however, it is a fatal flaw in a life being lived. Tower sees too much and, in seeing so clearly, wants too little. He could be a character from Greek myth: a man so gifted with vision that he is unable to abandon it and simply, irrationally desire anyone or anything. In the book, Tower is, as he would wish to be, barely perceptible, except through the workings of his exquisite eye.

The same might be said of Wescott the novelist, whose eye is so cold and precise, so hawklike, that the novel itself might suffer from an excess of clarity and a dearth of passion if it weren't redeemed by its language. Almost every page contains some small wonder of phrase or insight, some instance of the world keenly observed and reinvented. Of hunters near Alexandra's château, Wescott writes, "We could hear their hunting horns which sounded like a picnic of boy sopranos, lost." When Mrs. Cullen gives Tower the hawk to hold, briefly, on his wrist, we read, "At the least move her talons pricked the leather and pulled it a bit—as fashionable women's fingernails do on certain fabrics—though evidently she held them as loose and harmless as she could. Only her grip as a whole was hard, like a pair of tight, heated iron bracelets." Sentences like that are beauties in themselves, and the fact that they also serve the book's larger meanings can only be considered with an appreciation bordering on awe.

To my mind, *The Pilgrim Hawk* stands unembarrassed beside Ford Madox Ford's *The Good Soldier*, F. Scott Fitzgerald's *The Great Gatsby*, and Henry James's "The Aspern Papers." Those particular titles come to mind because they are all stories about disastrously intense passions and desires, narrated by someone untroubled by either, or, at best, by passions and desires that prove disastrously easy to manage. Each book offers, in one way or another, a narrative keyhole through which the reader is invited to peer at scandalous and salacious acts, and each implies that whatever cannot be seen through the keyhole is at least as significant as what can. Finally, each shares the conviction that, as far as human affairs are concerned, it may be better to live hugely and tragically, even in the service of some grand, ardent mistake, than submit to the seductions of mildness, reason, and order.

It is James, however, whom Wescott most nearly resembles. Ford and Fitzgerald produce their internal combustions at least in part by subjecting cosseted characters to ordained accidents, by creating collisions between comfort and chaos, but Wescott, like James, produces all his sparks from within: what fascinates him are devastating events that spring directly from character. *The Pilgrim Hawk* could be the work of a particularly brilliant clockmaker—a clockmaker capable of creating a mechanism of gears, springs, and pulleys that, when set in motion, obeys every known law of cause and effect but results, ultimately, in chaos. There is a sense, in Wescott as in James, that the mechanism requires no outside intervention: no matter how many times we wind the clock it will always tick along, with flawless precision, toward the same undoing.

The Pilgrim Hawk is, in short, a work of brilliance, and brilliance is not a word one often gets to apply to obscure books more than sixty years old. It was Wescott's third novel, following his well-received book *The Grandmothers*. He would publish one more, *Apartment in Athens*, in 1945, and then live another forty years publishing only essays and journals. There is, to my knowledge, little information about why he stopped writing fiction, though I tend to believe that writers who stop writing do so for reasons as ultimately mysterious as those that drove them to attempt writing in the first place. Whether the general neglect of Wescott's book stems from his long period of relative silence, or from the book's foreignness (it is a profoundly European book written by an American, and difficult to categorize), its stern and rather drab title (one wonders what would have happened to *The Great Gatsby* if Fitzgerald had obeyed his early inclination to call it *The High-Bouncing Lover*), or some more fundamental flaw in the world's ability to keep track of its gifts and glories, I can't help but believe that it will not only survive but, ultimately, prosper. Those of us who love books, as well as those of us who write them, are sometimes called upon for prodigious acts of patience.

ABOUT THE AUTHORS

MICHAEL CUNNINGHAM is the author of three novels: *A Home at the End of the World*, *Flesh and Blood*, and *The Hours*, which won the 1999 Pulitzer Prize for Fiction.

ARTHUR C. DANTO is the Johnsonian Professor of Philosophy Emeritus at Columbia University, art critic for *The Nation*, and author of many books about art and philosophy. He lives in Manhattan with his wife, Barbara Westman.

LYDIA DAVIS is the author of several works of fiction, including *Break It Down*, *The End of the Story*, and, most recently, *Samuel Johnson Is Indignant: Stories*.

EDWIN FRANK is the editor of NYRB Classics.

ELIZABETH HARDWICK was born in Lexington, Kentucky, and educated at the University of Kentucky and Columbia University. A recipient of a Gold Medal from the American Academy of Arts and Letters, she is the author of *Sleepless Nights* and two other novels, a biography of Herman Melville, and four collections of essays. Elizabeth Hardwick lives in New York City.

JONATHAN LETHEM is the author of *Motherless Brooklyn*

and four other novels, and the editor of *The Vintage Book of Amnesia*. He lives in Brooklyn and Toronto.

TONI MORRISON is the author of seven novels, among them *The Bluest Eye*, *Beloved*, *Jazz*, and *Paradise*. Born in Ohio and a graduate of Howard and Cornell, she is now Robert F. Goheen Professor at Princeton. In 1993 she won the Nobel Prize for Literature.

FRANCINE PROSE is the author of eleven works of fiction, including the National Book Award finalist *The Blue Angel*. Her stories and essays have appeared in numerous publications.

LUC SANTE is the author of *Low Life*, *Evidence*, and *The Factory of Facts*.

SUSAN SONTAG has written novels, stories, essays, and plays; written and directed films; and worked as a theater director in the United States and Europe. In 2001 she was awarded the Jerusalem Prize. Her most recent novel, *In America*, won the National Book Award for Fiction in 2000.

COLM TÓIBÍN's novels include *The Story of the Night* and *The Blackwater Lightship*, which was shortlisted for the Booker Prize in 1999. He is the editor of *The Penguin Book of Irish Fiction* and lives in Dublin.

JOHN UPDIKE was born in 1932 in Shillington, Pennsylvania.

In 1954 he began to publish in *The New Yorker*, to which he has contributed short stories, poems, and criticism. His novels have won the Pulitzer Prize, among other awards.

ELIOT WEINBERGER is the author of three collections of essays: *Outside Stories*, *Works on Paper*, and *Karmic Traces*. He is also the editor and translator of the *Collected Poems* of Octavio Paz and the *Selected Non-Fictions* of Jorge Luis Borges.

JAMES WOOD was born in Durham, England, in 1965 and attended Cambridge University. He is the author of *The Broken Estate: Essays on Literature and Belief* and *The Book Against God*, a novel.